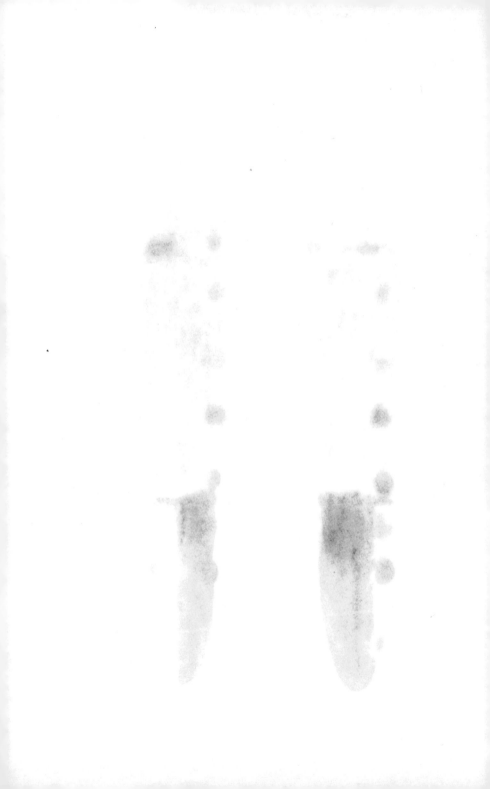

The Mountains West of Town

The Mountains West of Town

Warwick Downing

Saturday Review Press | E. P. Dutton & Co., Inc.

To Barbara

82 05275

My special thanks to Susan T. Smith, who wouldn't let it go until it was done; Charles Downing, for getting Garver out of jail; William Reiss, in lieu of money, for co-hosting the show; and Richard Downing, father and son, for their examples.

The
Mountains
West of Town

1

It was Saturday night. The mountains west of town were still silhouetted against a summer evening sky, which was pale on the horizon, but faded into bottom-of-the-ocean blue. I'd intended to drive on to my ranch on Shadow Mountain and don't even know why I stopped. It had been two weeks since I'd picked up the mail and another two weeks wouldn't have mattered.

The mail was in a loose pile on the floor of my office—what there was of it. Most of the letters I get I don't answer, which tends to cut into the volume after a while. There were one or two bills, which I put on the desk; several ads, which I dropped into the wastebasket; three legal periodicals that I decided to take with me; and several announcements from other lawyers. I opened them, glanced at them, and tossed them into the wastebasket next to the ads.

But one of them was an invitation to a party.

At one time I enjoyed parties, or thought I did, but now, to be perfectly frank, I think they're a pain in the ass. Merely dropping that card in the wastebasket didn't seem expressive enough; I started to tear it up; then noticed a note, scribbled on the bottom:

> I've been trying to call you, Mr. Tree, but
> you are never in. Please come. Something strange
> is going on and I need help.
> Phillip Garver

I'd never met Phillip Garver, but the prospect of him needing my help appealed to me. Some months before a feature article in the Denver *Chronicle* had compared our so-called careers. It claimed Garver was now for the Liberals what I myself had once been for the Conservatives, namely, a Rising Star on the Political Scene, and had gone on to pose the challenging question: "Will Phillip Garver take himself out of the running, just as Nathan Tree did more than a decade ago?"

It told of the time when I was Denver's District Attorney. But every precinct committeeman in the state knew I was really running for Governor, and after that, who knows? The next step on the road to glory should have been mayor of Denver, but I never took it. Instead I did what a lot of people do now, although then it was considered unusual. I dropped out.

"Tree became a hermit," the article claimed. "He still comes to Denver occasionally—long enough to buy supplies and get drunk—but his sympathies have taken quite a turn. Now he defends—successfully, if one can get him to take the case—the people he used to put away."

When the piece got around to comparing the young man to me, it claimed to find parallels between us "as eerily complete as those between Abraham Lincoln and John Kennedy"—thereby proving what I have always known, which is that newspaper reporters have about as much imagination as mules, and an identical capacity for making asinine remarks. Both Garver and I were native Coloradoans from wealthy, politically ambitious families with long traditions of public service, the article said. We had both attended Colorado University at Boulder, where each of us had distinguished himself scholastically and athletically. We had fought for our country, of course in different wars, but each with sufficient valor to have been decorated—although Garver had seen fit to return the medals. (I had snorted at that. The young pup probably had to pin back his hair before he could see well enough to find them.)

We were also both crusaders, the article claimed. I had been the fighting District Attorney after World War II who had battled for righteousness, law, and order; and Garver, as head of an environmentalist-action group called "Clear Sky," was engaged in fighting the powerful oil interests that (some will say) threaten life itself. But most strikingly, as with Abraham and John, both of us were possessed of those peculiarly attractive qualities that are collected under the heading of "charisma." We stood forth as living symbols of what was most admired in our respective day . . . At which point I had wadded the paper into a ball and tossed it out of my sight.

I looked at Garver's invitation again. The damned party apparently was in full swing at that very moment. "Shit." I didn't relish the thought of spending the night in Denver, which would mean no pine fire in the morning, no mountain sunrise, and no solitude. But I decided to go. I was curious about this young negative of me—or positive, depending on who did the developing—and wondered what could have happened to him to impel him to ask for help.

My "office" in Denver is actually an apartment with a desk in it, which I use as an office when in town. From the clothes I keep there I put on a blue suit with a thin green tie, then brushed my hair and trotted down two flights of stairs to my truck. It's a 1955 four-wheel-drive Jeep pickup and has managed to collect a few dents, but they don't bother the way it runs.

According to the invitation, I was to go to the Gates

Tower at 911 Grant. I'd never been there but had a hunch what it would look like, and was right. It was one of the new high-rise apartments on the south slope of Capitol Hill, thrust in amongst the fine old estates that rent rooms now, as offensive as a space ship in Eden. It even looked like a space ship. It was made of steel and glass and rested lightly on top of huge concrete pillars, as though in the process of blasting off.

Obviously Garver's apartment was too small to hold his friends, because when I got off the elevator there were young people even in the hall. They laughed, joked, and rattled ice cubes, vigorously pursuing their constitutional right to Happiness. Most of the men had wavy heads of hair and wore tooled leather boots, like Hollywood cowboys, and the young ladies wandered around with their bare legs hanging out. "I seem to have run into a party," I said to an expectant-looking fellow standing alone near the wall.

"Party is right, man. We beat the hell out of them! Have a drink!"

"I take it this is a celebration of some kind?"

"Damn right it is! Old man Dix is dead, and we did it! Sonuvabitch!" He raised the glass in his hand defiantly, as though to say, "Right on!"

"Old man Dix?"

"*You* know! The owner of Great Mesa Shale! The strip-mining land rapist in the Piceance Basin!" His eyes had glazed with some kind of ideological orgasm, and he seemed to be frothing at the mouth. "It's in all the papers, man!" he shouted.

The fellow may have been insane. I hoped so. It would explain his behavior. I decided to conduct my business as quickly as possible, and leave. "Could you point Phillip Garver out to me?"

He glared at me with suspicion. "Why? You an oil company spy or something?"

"No."

4

"Well he's around here someplace. Try that door over there." I nodded and opened the door to Garver's apartment.

There were fewer people there than in the hall and the talking was subdued by comparison, although still loud enough to scare the fish. I'd intended to dislike everything about the place, but found the room at least tolerable. It wasn't cluttered with furniture and what was there had a Western tone, like stepping into a ranch house in Wyoming. A small fire burned in the fireplace and sliding glass doors opened out onto a deck that overlooked a corner of town.

A young lady wearing an apron got in front of me. It's possible she had on more than that. "Hi," she said, completely oblivious to her indecency. "Can I get you a drink?"

I had to work my voice around the sudden lump in my throat. "No thanks."

Then a thin, oddly attractive woman in her middle thirties excused herself from the dominant group in the room and came over to greet me. She had large, brittle-looking breasts and the deep cleft between them was tanned to an Indian brown. "Hello," she said, smiling and extending her hand. "I'm Sharon Garver."

I avoid the use of my name, if possible. It saves a lot of questions. "Hello," I said, taking her hand and then trying to let go. But she hung on with the tenacity of the hostess, and I assumed she was Garver's wife. "I didn't know Garver was married."

"Phillip isn't," she said. "I'm Pete Garver's wife. Phil's older brother."

"Well, I'm glad to know you." I managed to get my hand out of there but she continued to stand in my way, like some kind of sentinel. "Is Phillip here?"

"Of course he is. Who are you?"

"Nathan Tree."

5

"Oh! How delightful to meet you, Mr. Tree! Can I get you something?"

"No thanks. I wonder though, if . . ."

"I've heard so much about you, especially after that article in the paper! But I always thought you were—well, not real. A legend or something." She blushed with the precision of someone who has practiced blushing before a mirror. "I hadn't realized you were—pardon the expression —'one of us,' either." She pronounced it "eye-ther." "Have you known Phil long?"

"I've never met him."

The group she had detached herself from had grown quiet, as had everyone else in the room. I could feel their eyes. "My husband isn't here. He'll be *terribly* disappointed not to have met you. But let me introduce you to . . ."

"Mr. Tree? Gee, I'm glad you came!"

A man I took to be Phillip Garver walked toward me. He was larger and heavier than me and his body had started to soften at the edges—mine has not—but his black hair wasn't too long, his clothes weren't too outlandish, and his face even showed a measure of strength and purpose. "Hey," he said, grinning around the silent room, "let's find a place we can talk."

I followed him through a sliding panel doorway that opened off the living room. There were two chairs, a large dresser, and a huge bed. A young couple sat on the bed, talking and smiling and gazing with foolish trust into each other's eyes.

The bed didn't look right, however. It squatted on the floor as though too heavy for its own legs, and was surrounded by heavy boards that held it together. "Is that a waterbed?" I asked.

"Yes. Don't tell my mother though. Okay?"

"Are they—I'll be damned—comfortable?"

"They really are. Like to sit on it?"

I did, and it didn't seem too sinful. Then I noticed the

couple on the other side, watching with the delight and solicitude of teenagers initiating an older person back to the joys of youth. It annoyed the hell out of me. I bounced on the thing, hoping to get a wave going that would roll them off, but it didn't work. "I don't hear any water lapping around in there," I said.

"Feels good though, doesn't it?"

"It would take some getting used to."

He grinned, which is something young people do a great deal. I think it has something to do with television. Then he shooshed the others out of the room, dragged up a chair, and sat down. "Thanks for coming, Mr. Tree. I didn't think you would."

"Why?"

"Politics, I guess."

"Politics! I don't give a rat's ass about politics!"

"I do, Mr. Tree," he said, like a magnificent young fool. "I believe in what I do. It isn't only so I can be President some day."

Oddly enough, I still admire such magnificent foolishness. "I believed once too, Phillip," I told him. "A different God perhaps, although it may have been just another side of the same one."

"What happened, Mr. Tree?"

"Some other time. And would you mind calling me Nathan instead of Mr. Tree? What if some dog were to hear you?" He grinned again. "Now suppose you tell me what this is all about."

"Well, I have a—a girl friend, I guess you'd call her. Anyway, she lives with me."

"A lover?"

"We aren't really lovers. It isn't that big a deal."

The word *lover* apparently has undergone some refinements since I was a young man. "Go on."

"Monday night she disappeared. Just like that. I had to go out around ten and she was here when I left, but when

7

I got back around midnight, she was gone. I haven't heard a word from her since."

"Maybe she got tired of waiting."

"Maybe. But I think something's happened."

"Why do you think so?"

"The reason I went out that night was because of a telephone call that never did sound right. Some character . . ."

"Skip that for now. What did you do?"

"Drove to Castle Rock to meet the guy that called—it only took forty-five minutes—but no one was there."

"The young lady was gone when you got back?"

"Yes. Except her clothes are still here. So's her jewelry, her books, her perfumes and stuff—everything." His body seemed to tighten with concern.

"What about her purse?"

"Gone."

"Did she have money in it?"

"Probably. She always had lots of money."

"What's her name?"

"Well—her real one, or the one she uses?" he asked.

"You tell me."

His head moved slowly back and forth, as though shaking it might somehow fill it with sense. "Her real name is Cora Shannon and she's actually a petroleum geologist for the Dolores Petroleum Company, but I'm the only one around here who knows. Everybody thinks she's just a student named JoAnn White."

"Why the big mystery?"

"You've got to understand my situation, Nathan. The people I work with aren't very willing to compromise. On anything. If they'd known who she really was, they'd have killed her."

"Do you mean that?"

"Well—no."

"Was she with you for some reason other than . . ."

"Yes. Her company's been looking for a good oil shale

8

property and the outfit we just beat—now they've been beaten—are pretty discouraged."

"Go through it again, with names."

He glanced around the room, as though to make sure we were alone. "All right. Mainly because of the help we got from JoAnn, we just beat an oil shale developer in court. Maybe you read about it."

"Great Mesa Shale?"

"Yes. Anyway, the Dolores Petroleum Company has been trying to buy Great Mesa's land for two years, and now it looks like they'll be able to."

"What good would it do Dolores to buy it? Wouldn't you shut them down too?"

"We'd try. But if they went about it right, there wouldn't be much we could do. We've fairly well faced up to the fact we can't keep the oil companies out. All we can do is compel them to use certain environmental safeguards."

"Why won't Great Mesa do it right?"

He made a face that apparently was intended to explain something. "It's owned by a Neanderthal nut by the name of Robert Dix. He bought up the land in 1950 for about ten dollars an acre—before people knew we'd have to go to oil shale some day, which is something he predicted—but he says if he can't mine it the way he wants, the hell with it. He'll sell out."

I'd heard of Robert Dix. At one time the oil business had been peopled with eccentrics, and Dix was generally regarded as a throwback. "Let me see if I've got it right," I said. "Dolores Petroleum actually wanted Great Mesa to lose the lawsuit, hoping they'd be able to buy the property?"

"Yes."

"So they loaned the girl to you?"

"That's right."

"However, you wanted to keep her identity a secret—and I suppose Dolores Petroleum did too, didn't they? I

9

don't imagine they wanted Dix to know what they were doing?"

"Right again."

"What kind of money is involved?" I asked.

"Millions, which is one of the reasons I'm worried. Dix could sell what he's got to one of the majors right now for fifty million dollars, and Dolores offered him fifty-five before the lawsuit."

"That's a lot of money for a few acres of land."

"Twenty-five hundred acres," Garver said. "With anywhere from half a billion to a billion barrels of oil in it. Comes out to about ten cents a barrel."

Something seemed to touch my leg as I sat on the bed. I turned around, patting the water mattress. "What is it?" Garver asked.

"Nothing." I rubbed my hand along the line of my jaw, trying to form an impression of what I'd heard. "She's been gone since Monday night, and so has her money?"

"Yes."

"When was the hearing?"

"You mean the trial with Great Mesa? Wednesday. I thought we'd been double-crossed, but . . ."

"By the girl?"

He nodded. "I halfway expected her to turn up as one of their witnesses."

"But it went favorably for you, I take it?"

"Couldn't have gone better. She'd really done a job— breaking our testimony down into simple English, educating us first as to the meaning of a lot of technical gibberish; we were ready for them and it showed. The judge ruled in our favor."

"Have you called Dolores Petroleum about her? Maybe she went back to work."

"I tried that. They gave me some song and dance about how she's been gone over three months on a sabbatical leave, and they don't know where she is."

"What about the police? Have you called them?"

"No. The only other person I've talked to is Gene Car-ruthers."

"Who is he?"

"Kind of a goofy guy. Calls himself a 'psychological engineer.' He lives in the building."

"Why did you call him?"

"Well, JoAnn seemed nervous about my leaving her alone that night. So I called Carruthers and asked him to stay with her until I got back."

"Did he?"

"He was in the middle of a TV show but said he'd come up when it was finished. So I left. When I got back and no-body was here, I thought they were down in his apart-ment, so I went down to get her."

"And?"

"Gene told me he came up, but she wouldn't answer the door. He even telephoned a couple of times, but no an-swer. He thought she'd gone to bed."

"Does he have any idea where she is?" I asked.

"He has an idea. He thinks she's trying to make me miss her so I'll marry her."

"Anything else?"

"Just little things, Nathan. When I got back that night the place looked—touched, somehow. I can't explain it. I'm sure the bed had been moved, for example. I read a lot in bed and the lamp on the wall above wasn't centered right. The bathroom wasn't right, either. Some wet towels were hanging in there, which is something JoAnn just never did. After she used a towel, she'd toss it in the hamper. And in the kitchen there's a knife rack above the stove. She is so neat about things, but here this knife was, lying on the counter."

"Bloody?"

"No. Just out."

I wished I'd gone on to my ranch. "What do you want from me, Phillip? Legal advice or a piece of my mind?"

"I don't know. I've heard you help people sometimes. Maybe you can find out what happened to her."

"You're sure all her clothes are here?"

"Yes. Even the ones she had on Monday night."

"It's obvious then," I said. "She took her purse and went for a stroll in the nude. She just hasn't gotten back."

"It isn't funny to me, Nathan. I'm really worried."

"Well, Phillip, you seem to think you're caught in the middle of some huge conspiracy. But the way you young people drift through each other now—this obscene willingness to make love without touching—what can you expect? I think she got tired of waiting for you and left."

He stared at me, then got to his feet. "Sorry to have bothered you," he said. But it sounded like: "Go to hell." Then he stuck out his hand and grinned. "Thanks for coming, though. I've wanted to meet you a long time."

"Wait a minute," I said. It was too late to go home that night anyway, and I found that I liked the young man. "That's just an impression. Mind if I hang around?"

He grinned again. "I sure don't," he said. "Eggs for breakfast."

2

As a general rule, older people should not attend parties given by the young—unless they enjoy being drowned in oceans of virtue. In the course of a very few hours, I was subjected to enough High Ideals and Intelligent Solutions to take care of all the problems of the world for the next thousand years. I was also instructed as to the name of the Enemy.

Oil derricks are phallic symbols, a young lady informed me, and I was invited to draw my own conclusions as to gushers. And whereas in my ignorance I had always believed Nazism was a scourge and the underworld was peopled by evil men, I was advised that nothing could compare with the oil industry.

A mere handful of large companies had a stranglehold on the world, a serious fellow who lisped thought I should know. These companies manipulated the economies of the various nations with the arrogance and selfishness of the Krupps. In concert with other cartels and monopolies, they'd created a totally unjustified dependence on their product—namely, petroleum—and they greedily stuffed their pockets with money as they mercilessly gutted the earth of its natural resources.

Somehow, I managed to tease this roomful of young

13

Christians into casting me as Defender of the Right. "Come on, Mr. Tree," a young lady said. Her skirt came all the way over her rump as long as she stood up straight, and she always seemed to catch me staring at her legs. "You don't believe that crap, do you? How *can* you?"

"Come on, Miss Robinson," I said. "Tell me why I shouldn't believe it? Your reason for disbelieving it seems to be the police say it's true, which automatically makes it a lie."

We had gotten off the subject of oil and had started to argue about the recent murder of a black man named Watt Chambers. His body had been found Monday night —it occurred to me, the same night Cora Shannon or JoAnn White, or whatever the hell her name was, had disappeared—and according to the authorities he'd been executed by a black militant group he belonged to.

But the young woman could not accept the obvious, and her voice became a snarl. "Don't mock me," she said—and suddenly I wanted to stop. I could feel it coming, like a prerecorded scene—an ugliness etched by someone onto the tape—and I wanted to turn the damned machine off. "Didn't you hear about that phony note with his body?"

I tried to smile. "Said 'Death to the Infidel,' didn't it?"

"Well, what more proof can you possibly need than that? You don't think black militants talk like *that*?"

"I don't know any black militants. But the police . . ."

"The police. *Fuck* the police!"

I don't know what happened to me then. At times an awful stillness will get a grip on me, and it formed around me then like a castle wall. "Why should you be surprised, Miss Robinson?" I said. "That's the way those niggers are."

"Ah!" She stared at me in disgust. "Are you trying to be funny?"

"I don't know. Were you?"

"I object most strenuously to that term!"

"Fuck, or nigger?"

14

It had gotten quiet in the room, and she stared at me as though I had perhaps ten seconds to change my mind. "Let's get back to the point, if you don't mind."

"By all means."

"Mr. Tree, do you honestly think any black organization would leave a note like that?"

"Why not? Black extremists are like all other extremists, aren't they? And don't all of them like to shroud their killings with grand design and noble purpose?"

"Oh!"

"I admire them, in fact," I said. "They have the ability to make very ordinary murders look as though they were done for reasons."

"This isn't funny," she said. "I knew Watt. He was a gentle, truly wonderful person. And now to have you make jokes about him . . ."

"You're right. There must be other murders that are funnier."

She put her drink on a coffee table and walked away. I watched her legs and then drained the glass in my hand. Backs all around the room were turned toward me and I felt better, all alone.

"You shouldn't have done that, Mr. Tree."

I turned around and confronted Gene Carruthers, a thoughtful-looking, bespectacled fellow that Garver had introduced me to earlier. He was the so-called psychological engineer, and I had noticed how he had spent a good share of the night observing me. "My aggressive impulses must have gotten the upper hand," I said.

He smiled at me with tolerance and understanding. "You seem to have your share of aggressive impulses—which is unfortunate, really. There are so many new, exciting techniques now. Even my little company has been involved with some of them—psycho-technological applications of various chemicals—fascinating field. Fascinating."

It was obvious he had a solution of some kind to the problem, whatever it was. "Go ahead."

15

"You know, in this time, there is simply no reason for a person to—to spend his life with his insides tied in knots." He smiled again and I lifted a glass off the waitress's passing tray. "Don't you agree?"

"I think you're trying to manipulate me."

"Possibly so. Possibly so. But I've watched you and you seem so—unhappy—and of course there's this legend, really, that has built up around you. The world at your feet and you drop out, sort of thing. You seem such a lonely man, Mr. Tree. It's all so unnecessary."

"'Psycho-technological application of various chemicals,'" I said. "Does that mean pills?"

"Well, yes. It does."

"Didn't I hear someone say you're experimenting with a drug that's supposed to suppress aggressive behavior?"

"Whatever you may think, Mr. Tree, I am not insane. But if we don't do something soon, on a national level, to reduce tensions, we are apt to blow up the world."

"What a loss," I said. "Where would Mankind be?"

From a distance I somehow became aware of Sharon Garver and her brittle breasts, which seemed to push themselves between Carruthers and me even though she was on the other side of the room. Her husband was not at the party, and Phillip's girl friend wasn't there either. Sharon had assumed the role of hostess with uncommon ease. "Come on, everyone!" she called loudly. "To the waterbed!" She extended an arm as though leading a charge, and advanced with an army from the kitchen. "You too, Nathan," she commanded, taking my hand and leading me into the bedroom. "I have a bet with Phil and you can help me win some money!"

The others crowded in the room behind us as Sharon took off her shoes and stepped on the bed. She was awkward, as though standing for the first time on a trampoline, then let go of my hand and took an experimental step toward the middle. Carefully she began to bounce on the mattress. "Hey, guys," she cried, her voice wavering be-

16

tween gaiety and fear. "You can help me win ten dollars. I'll split it with you!"

"Big deal," someone said. "A nickel apiece."

"Listen to me!" she called. "Everyone here knows what a big mouth Phil has. Right?"

"Right!"

"Well, our famous leader told me this waterbed is strong enough to hold *all* of us at one time! I told him to put his money where his mouth is—and he did! Now all we have to do is climb on, break it open, and flood the place!" She did a little step, like a witch around a cauldron. "Take your shoes off, though. It isn't fair just to punch holes in it."

They all thought it was fun and in a second or two all the shoes were off, except mine. They crowded onto the mattress. "You too, Nathan," Sharon said, struggling for the edge and reaching out her hand. "Don't you want to fall in and be a wet blanket like everyone else?"

"No."

"Hey. This is groovy," one of them said. "What about a little ol' mass love-in?"

"Don't be old-fashioned."

"That's old-fashioned?"

"When will it break, Sharon?"

"I don't *know*," she said, perplexed. "You don't suppose he was *right* about something?"

"You know, I can feel something—there!" one of the men said. "Feel it? What's Phil-baby got in here?"

"A porpoise, probably. They're so ecological."

"Feels like a body. Anybody missing?" someone said, and laughed.

A sudden weight pushed on my stomach. I watched as Sharon, obviously curious, told everyone to get off the bed and began stripping away the sheets and covers. "What are you keeping in here, Phillip?"

Phillip Garver grinned around the room. He seemed

to have gotten drunk. "I don't know what the hell you're . . ."

When the last sheet was off, we could see it. A large shadow rippled softly under the surface of the plastic material. The lines were not distinct, but it looked like the silhouette of a woman, floating on her back, her legs slightly apart and her arms drifting away from her sides.

3

The shadow dipped slowly out of sight like a fish, hunting the bottom of the pool. Sharon Garver tried to scream, then dropped to the floor like a puppet with no support. "Take it easy. Everyone take it easy," I said, trying to keep my voice calm. "Somebody give me a hand." I took Sharon under her arms and a young man grabbed her by the ankles, and we lugged her into the living room and laid her on the couch. "You girls keep her warm, will you? Coats, blankets, anything." I went back to the bedroom.

No one could talk, which was a blessing. Four or five of them sat on the floor with their heads between their legs, and I could hear someone in the bathroom, throwing up. "I'm leaving," one of the men suddenly announced. "Yeah. Me too," another one said. "Just get in the way." The two wavy-headed cowboys looked at no one as they stumbled out the door. A few others mumbled apologies of some sort and followed.

Garver had slumped in a chair. "Get up, Phillip," I said, but he didn't hear. I grabbed his shoulders and shook him until he brushed away my hands. "Get up," I told him. "Go to the kitchen and fix coffee."

"Okay."

Then a young jackass stormed into the room with a

bread knife in his hand. He raised it over the waterbed.

"*Don't* do that!" I yelled.

"Let me go!" he shouted. "I'm going to get her out of there!"

I reached over the top of his head, grabbed his nose, and threw him out of the way. "Get that knife," I said to Miss Robinson, who watched as numb as a zombie as the knife clattered to the floor. "You," I said to the idiot on the floor. "Instead of behaving like a jackass, why don't you call the police?"

"Yeah. Okay."

I got everyone out of the bedroom and shut the door behind us. "You and you," I said to the two biggest men in the room. "Don't let anyone in there until the police get here."

"Sure, Mr. Tree."

Someone asked if she could leave and I told her no one could make anyone stay. They started trickling out after that. I wished all of them would go, but knew better than to suggest it. I went to the kitchen and found Garver sitting on a stool trying to sip a cup of coffee. Miss Robinson stood nearby with the bread knife still clutched in her hand. "Has he said anything?"

"No. He can't seem to talk."

"Just as well," I said, taking the knife and putting it on the counter. "He may have noble ideals, but he isn't particularly bright."

"What?"

"Leave us alone, will you, Miss Robinson? I'd like to talk to him."

"Of course."

"Phillip, listen to me."

"I'm listening."

"Did you do this?"

"No."

"How the hell did her body get in the waterbed?"

"It could be done," he said.

"How?"

"Cut a hole in it and then seal up the hole."

"Damn it. How would you seal up the hole?"

"Repair kit." He barely had the breath to say it.

"Do you have one?"

He nodded.

"Where?"

"The linen closet."

"Show me," I said.

"God. Can't we wait till they leave?"

"No. I want to see it before the police get here."

He got to his feet. His face was as white as a fresh blaze on a tree, and I had to hold him up as we pushed our way through the stillness of the living room. Sharon Garver was still stretched out on the couch and breathing, but other than that she looked dead. "For God's sake, get a doctor!" I said to one of the girls.

"Oh. Who?"

The female was on her feet, but looked as though she could use a doctor too. "I don't know. Call her husband."

"Can't," Phillip mumbled. "Snowmass Lake, on a climb."

"What about Carruthers?"

"He left," the girl said.

"Well, get someone!" I said. "And don't let her up when she comes to. Get some whisky in her first."

We came to the bedroom door. "You can't go in," one of the two mooses said.

"What?"

"You said don't let anyone in until the police get here, Mr. Tree."

"Move, you big idiot."

Garver opened the door. "One of you come with us," I said. "I want you to see what we do."

The linen closet was on the wall between the waterbed and the bathroom. It was behind a plate-glass mirror door about five feet tall and a foot and a half wide. Garver

21

started to reach for the handle and I stopped him, opened the blade on my knife, and wedged the door open from the bottom. "Is the kit there?" I asked.

"Yes." He sounded ready to throw up. "Second shelf from the top."

I saw a cardboard box about six inches high and nine inches wide that said, "Earth People Water Products of Colorado." Under the inscription was the photograph of a water mattress filled with water with an Army tank balanced on top. "If it will hold a tank, it ought to hold you," a caption under the photograph read. "Look carefully, Phillip, but don't touch anything. Not even a shelf."

He started to lean on one and I brushed his hand away. "Didn't you understand me?"

"I—yes." He bent toward the shelf with the kit on it, holding my arm.

"Is anything different from the way you remember it?"

"I don't know. I don't think so." He straightened up and let go of me.

"When was the last time you got something out of here?" I asked. A police siren had started to cut the night.

"At least a month ago."

"That long since you changed the linen or got a towel?"

"Cora did all that stuff."

"As near as you can remember, is the kit where you left it?"

"Yes."

"All right. Let's go." I had to take him by the arm again, and started pulling him out. "All we did in there was look. Right?" I said to the blond-headed giant who had come with us.

"Yes, sir. You didn't touch a thing."

I took Phillip back to the kitchen, where some people had gathered to talk. Two of them looked away when they saw Phillip and one of them glared at us harshly. I recognized their expressions. I'd seen the same hard faces on hundreds of jurors, and knew their verdict was "guilty."

"Leave us alone, please," I said, and they marched angrily out of the room.

Garver sat on a kitchen stool and let his head droop. "The police will question you, Phillip. Tell them you respectfully decline to answer their questions on the advice of your lawyer."

"All right."

"For all we know, this is a joke," I said, watching him carefully.

His head snapped up. "What do you mean?"

"That may be a dummy in the waterbed."

"You think so? God. You think so?"

We heard a commotion in the living room and a moment later a uniformed policeman stuck his head into the kitchen. "You Phillip Garver?" he said to me.

"No. This man here."

"I got to talk to him, mister. You'll have to leave."

"Sorry," I said. "I'm a lawyer, this man is my client, and I'm staying."

"You don't have the right, mister. He isn't even a suspect."

"He will be, soon enough."

"You're under arrest for obstruction of justice."

"Who's in charge of homicide investigations now? Charlie Riggs?" I asked.

"That don't make any difference whatsoever."

"Just do me a favor before you arrest me. Check with him. Okay?"

He hesitated. "Okay. I got enough to do now anyway. But don't either of you gentlemen go until I or Lieutenant Riggs says so." He left.

Garver had come back to life and prowled the kitchen like a panther in a cage. "I hope you're right about it being a dummy," he said. "God, I hope you're right."

I poured coffee. "Don't count on it."

"I've been sleeping on that waterbed since Monday. Why didn't I feel her?"

23

I remembered sitting on the thing earlier and something touching my leg. "People aren't aware of what they don't expect, Phillip."

He dropped to the stool and drank more coffee. "Some joke. Some fucking joke."

"When Riggs gets here, I'll have to leave you alone," I said.

"How come?"

"I want to tell him about that repair kit and see what he does."

"I'll be all right."

"You'll probably be guarded by a cop. He'll advise you of your rights and then go right on asking questions, even after you've said you don't want to talk. Don't say anything then, either. Understand?"

"Yes."

"If it's a body and not a dummy in the waterbed, you'll probably be booked tonight for murder."

He nodded.

"If that happens I'll talk to you in the morning."

"All right."

"Between now and then, start remembering. Everything you can think of about the girl. Exactly what happened Monday night. And who could have done this, and why."

"Okay."

"Don't write anything down. And don't talk it over with anyone but me."

"Especially don't do that," someone standing behind me said. I turned and saw Charlie Riggs. "Thought it might be you," he said. "I got enough troubles now."

"Hello, Charlie," I said. The larger man hadn't changed since the last time I'd seen him, two years before. His shoulders were as round and he might have been chewing on the same cigar. When I was DA, he had been my chief investigator, but he transferred to the police department when I resigned.

24

He didn't ask Garver any questions, but when I followed him into the bedroom he nodded at a detective who ambled into the kitchen, and I hoped Phillip would remember what I'd said. I told Charlie about the repair kit and he secured the linen closet for the lab crew and put the kit in a plastic bag. His photographers took pictures of the waterbed and the shadow, which had reappeared. Now it seemed to be sleeping on its side.

On top of the mattress, about twenty inches from the foot end, he pointed to where the plastic-like skin had been cut. The gash was four feet long and a strip of identical material had been pasted somehow over the cut. "Twenty people on that mattress?" he asked me.

"At least."

"How the hell did it hold?"

"According to the advertisement, it'll hold a tank."

When the coroner got there, they discussed the best way to get the body out. Finally Charlie ordered his men to open the valve at the top left-hand corner of the bed and drain out some water, which was put in a special container to be analyzed by the lab. Then the valve was closed and four men got on the bed, gently walking the shadow toward an edge. The shape rolled slowly ahead of their advancing feet and when it had been herded into the right place, they got off.

Charlie likes to know how things are done. He took a knife and jabbed it through the top, then drew it four feet along the edge. "How come that water don't come out?" he asked. The mattress skin didn't even sink, although water began to seep through the cut as it settled into the water.

"No pressure behind it, Lieutenant," one of the men said. "It's like a big bathtub."

The room filled with a putrid smell, like oil washed over a beach. The skin of the mattress seemed to stick to the water but finally a couple of men got it up and an air space formed over the body. A bluish sheen on the water made

25

delicate swirls. "Needs a bigger cut, Lieutenant," one of the men said, and Charlie dutifully extended the gash another two feet. Then very carefully the men from the coroner's office slid the nude, swollen body of a woman out of the mattress and onto a stretcher, covering her loosely with plastic. Her skin was the color of white paper, and she looked very cold.

Sharon Garver stood by the door, holding the wall for support. "My God," I heard her say. "It's JoAnn."

They took Garver to the police building and I drove to my apartment, letting the cool night air blow against my face. A slice of moon showed white against the sky and the lights of Green Mountain, a subdivision west of town on a foothill that used to be a cattle ranch, twinkled like stars. The lights lined asphalt streets, cut out of what had once been good grass land; but at night they looked like ornaments on a Christmas tree.

I keep whisky in the medicine chest in the bathroom, and poured myself a glass. When I lifted it my eyes slid across the mirror over the sink, and I threw the glass at it. My face shattered and fell off the wall. Good Lord, Hamlet, I thought, loosening my tie and picking up the bottle and trudging off to the bedroom. Now you're going to let it Get You Down.

There was no use trying to sleep, because Timothy Pettersenn III was back in my mind. I stripped to my shorts, stepped out of the heap of clothes on the floor, and propped myself in bed with the bottle.

It occurred to me I'd been dodging him most of my life. In grade school his mother and mine decided we should be friends, because after all *they* were friends; but the little four-eyed bastard gave me the creeps. He had the kind of smile that made you wonder if he knew of a peephole into the girls' toilet, and it got more mysterious as he got older.

And it's his smile that keeps crawling through my mind. I saw it twelve years ago, when he was strapped in the death chair at Canon City—and then about a year later I saw it again. I was in the middle of a speech—a thumper on Law and Order—and there was Timothy, standing in the crowd, smiling at me.

The little shit. I took another drag from the bottle and wished the whisky would do its job, and blank me out. My father may have wanted me to be President, but I'm not sure I ever really cared.

I just wished to Christ that four-eyes would let go.

4

I woke up the next morning, stuck out my tongue, and scratched it. It felt like some spiders had laced it with webs. Somehow I got in the shower and let cold water burn my skin, then shaved, dressed, and forced down two cups of coffee.

The police building looked out of place in the bright morning light, like a yellow scow stuck in the desert. Garver would be kept there until after his arraignment, then transferred to the county jail; and I looked beyond the nicotine-colored pile of brick to the cool blue mountains that were part of the sky, and wondered what the hell I was doing in town.

It was Sunday and I had to wait half an hour to see Garver. Finally a police cadet ushered me into a small gray-walled visitors' room. A square table stood in the center with a chair on either side, and a piece of sunlight from a small window put a yellow patch on the wall. A moment later a tough, beefy cop led Garver into the room, unhandcuffed him, then nodded at me and pulled the door shut as he left.

Garver no longer looked like The Leader. His skin had no color and when he tried to grin, it broke through his face like a tear in a curtain. "You'd think I killed somebody," he said, rubbing his wrists and dropping into the chair across from mine.

"Odd that you'd bring that up," I said, "just when I've been thinking maybe you should get someone else."

"What the hell are you talking about?"

"There are lots of lawyers in Denver, Phillip. I know a man who can speak for hours on any subject under the sun, and the less he knows about it, the more persuasive he is."

"So?"

"He's gifted. I'm not."

"From what I hear, you do all right."

"Yes, I do all right. But I don't have one of those powerful mouths. I'm forced to depend on the facts." He said nothing. "Have you thought about hiring a more gifted man?"

He glared at me with the harsh reality of a horse who has tried to stand on a broken leg. "I didn't kill her."

I tried to be gentle. "You're talking to an old DA," I said. His jaw got tight and his eyes dropped out of sight. "In that office, you learn to look at the facts. Want to hear some of them?" He didn't move, so I kept on talking. "The young female employee of an oil company is given a very unusual assignment. Along the way she becomes the earthmate of the Champion of the Environmentalists. Then last night her body is found inside the champion's waterbed. To a suspicious mind like mine, that raises a few questions."

"I sure as hell hope so."

"For example, whoever put her there had to know how."

"The directions are simple, Nathan. Anyone who can read could have done it."

"Provided they had the foresight to bring a repair kit with them, or knew where you kept yours. And provided they had lots of time."

"I told you about that telephone call. I was gone two hours, which would have been plenty of time."

29

"My point is, you had the time too." He glared toward the window. "But the hard question—especially for an ex-DA—is why would anyone bury her in *your* waterbed, in *your* apartment, anyway? Why go to such monumental lengths, just to kill?"

"Don't you see, Nathan? It had to have been a nut, and *I'm not a nut.*"

"I believe I'll reserve my judgment. But for the sake of argument, let's assume you're not a nut. Putting your friend there would give you plenty of time to figure out a way to get rid of her."

"Damn you. If you want out, why not just say, 'I quit'?"

I tried to read the expression on his face. "I don't want out, Phillip. But I'm telling you this. If you did it, get that other kind of lawyer."

"I didn't do it."

It's probably a sign of senility, I thought. At any rate, I believed him. "All right. Let's get down to it, then. Could the waterbed have been sealed without a repair kit?"

"I don't think so. Did it have a patch?"

"Yes. Out of the same material the mattress is made of."

"It was sealed with a repair kit, then."

"How do they work?"

"The kits have a roll of mattress cover about ten feet long and an inch and a half wide, and they also have what they call a 'dialectric sealer.'"

"Which is?"

"It looks like an electric razor. You make sure there isn't any moisture around the cut, then lay on a piece of roll and go over it with the sealer. 'Molecular excitation,' or something like that, fuses them together."

"Well enough to hold twenty people?"

"It's as strong as anywhere else on the bed, and those beds'll hold a tank. The manufacturer uses the same process on the seams."

"Are all waterbeds the same?"

"No. They're as different as cars."

30

"Would a repair kit from another model work on yours?"

"I doubt it. Most of them don't have repair kits anyway."

I wandered over to the small window at the end of the room and stared down into an outdoor exercise area, about the size of a cell. "When did you first meet JoAnn, or Cora, or whatever her name was?"

"About two months ago. Just after Great Mesa Shale had started strip-mining that land. We knew we had to stop them, but didn't know how."

"She told you?"

"Not quite. Our lawyers had already gotten a temporary restraining order when JoAnn happened along. She seemed to know exactly what was going on."

"And you were suspicious?"

"Damn right. Until she told me who she was."

A black prisoner walked into the courtyard below and started tossing a tennis ball against the wall. The fellow looked tired and hot. "What made you suspicious?"

"Too—providential, or something. She seemed too experienced to be a geology student. And her attitude wasn't strong enough. She didn't think of oil companies as the enemy. So I started following her and one afternoon she put on dark glasses and a wig, and I thought, aha! Then she drove to the Oilmen Club Building on Arapahoe, which is where Great Mesa is! I grabbed her when she came out and asked her what the hell was going on."

"She told you?"

"She did more than that. The Dolores Petroleum offices are in there too, and she took me back and introduced me to William Drake. He's the president—young guy, my age —and I got good vibes from him. He told me who JoAnn really was, what she was doing, and why. Said she'd done a lot of work on Dix's land and knew it as well as anyone. Including Dix."

"Dix is the owner of Great Mesa?"

31

"Yes."

"Why had JoAnn worked for him?"

"She hadn't. But Dolores Petroleum has been interested in that property a long time, and Dix let JoAnn do a survey to see what it was worth."

"Is it valuable?"

"Not as rich as Dix thinks, but good enough for Drake. If he can get it at the right price."

"Go on."

"Well, Drake told me a lot of people in the oil business were sore as hell at Dix because what he was doing was so flagrant. It was, too. He was strip-mining along the rim of a canyon, dumping the shale into a portable retort, and filling the canyon with spent shale. Ugly as hell. Drake couldn't say so publicly—oil people hang together, like doctors and lawyers—but what Dix was doing was bad for the industry."

"And Drake is such a loyal, public-minded oilman he wanted to help the industry. Is that it?"

"He didn't make any bones about it, Nathan. He was really after the land, and said so."

"Did JoAnn—Cora—know Dix?"

"Yes. She liked him, in fact. He's one of those pioneer types who think they should be able to do exactly what they want with their land, and to hell with the rest of the world."

The black man in the exercise area turned suddenly and threw the tennis ball over the wall. Then he sat down on the ground and buried his head in his arms. I wondered if the fellow had done it, whatever it was. I hoped so, as long as he'd been jailed for it. "Dolores Petroleum wanted to keep Cora Shannon's identity a secret so Dix wouldn't know how he was being double-crossed. Right?"

"I wanted to keep her identity a secret too. I'm willing to take help wherever I can get it, but some of the people on my staff aren't. If they'd known she was connected with an oil company they'd have . . ."

32

"Killed her?"

"That's just a figure of speech. But they wouldn't have liked it."

I came back to the table and sat down. "When did the girl move in with you?"

"Two months ago. About a week after she introduced me to Drake."

"How did you manage them both?"

"What the hell are you talking about now?" he asked.

"Sharon Garver."

He stared at me. "You know about that? How?"

It was just a guess, but I didn't burden him with that. "She's a witch, and witches project that kind of thing. They stake out their victims, or possessions, or lovers—it doesn't matter what you call them—and it stuck out all over her last night." He didn't look very comfortable, but I didn't mind making him squirm. It must be my nature. "What was Sharon to you, Phillip? A lover or another earthmate?"

"You'd have to call her a lover, I guess. She wouldn't have it any other way."

"What do you mean by that?"

He scratched his forehead. "I don't know exactly. She's older or something. Can't mess around just for the hell of it."

"You'd better tell me about it."

"Why? Sharon isn't involved in this thing."

"She led the parade onto the waterbed." His mouth hung open as though he'd been shot in the back. "Last night she made it sound like a bet. How did the subject come up?"

"We were in the kitchen, a bunch of us, kidding around . . ." A realization of some kind wrinkled his face. "She and I spent a lot of time on that waterbed," he said. "Then last night, in front of all those people, she started joking about the damn thing—what if it broke while I was

33

'searching for oil'—and before I knew it we'd made the bet."

"How long has it been going on between you?"

"A year and a half. I never could seem to end it."

"Why?"

"I don't know. Maybe she really is a witch. I know she scares the hell out of me."

"Did you always meet at your apartment?"

"No. She liked the waterbed but she liked hotels, too. All that intrigue turned her on."

"Did anyone else know about it?"

"Nobody. Wait. JoAnn did. Sharon called a few times and JoAnn answered the phone, and she kind of guessed. She thought it was funny."

"So you told her about it?"

"Yeah. She was real easy to talk to."

"Did Sharon have a key?" I asked.

"Two keys. One for the main door and one for the apartment."

"Were they copies?"

"Yes."

"And she could have made copies from them?"

"I don't see why not."

"Did you give keys to anyone else?"

"My brother had a set. But he gave them back a long time ago."

"You gave him one so he could visit his wife?"

Garver cleared his throat. "No. He had a little thing going for a while, but all it did was make him nervous. He's older too, I guess."

"After JoAnn moved in, what happened?"

He shrugged. "She did the cooking and I did the dishes. We made love, went to movies, worked on the case." His voice drifted to a halt and suddenly his face fell apart. He jumped up and turned his back to me.

I'll be damned, I thought. He's young enough to cry.

34

"Sorry," he said, still facing the wall. "I didn't get much sleep last night."

"I can come back."

"That's all right."

"Were you in love?"

"A little."

"What was she like?"

"Distant at first. Unattainable. Goal-oriented, if you know what I mean. But after I got to know her—wild, and soft—a real animal. And we fit." His face started to work again but he got it under control. "Built, too. I miss her."

My mouth felt dry and I found myself thinking about a cool glass of whisky over ice. "Monday night was the last time you saw her?"

"Yeah."

"Tell me about Monday. The whole day."

"We woke up about six and went out on the porch. It's real pretty in the morning—bright and clean, before all that exhaust spoils it—and we enjoyed it a while, then went back to bed."

"And?"

"We made love. Then about seven we got up and showered and had breakfast."

"After that?"

"We got dressed. I went to the office and she stayed in the apartment, said she'd be down later."

"Where is your office?"

"Fourteen ninety-nine Pike Street. An old mansion, made over into offices."

"Did she come down?"

He nodded. "About ten thirty. Quieter than usual. One of our lawyers was there, working with a witness. She sat in on it, helped with the coaching, asked the kinds of questions we thought they would ask and gave the answers. But something was bothering her. I asked her at lunch and she smiled at me and said, 'Nothing.'" He snuffled a moment, then wiped his nose. "I knew what was wrong, I

35

thought. Our little happening was over. The trial was two days away and after that she'd go back to work for that crummy oil company, and I'd keep on campaigning for the Senate. Our bodies fit but our life styles didn't, or some damn thing." He pulled out a handkerchief and blew his nose. "Kind of the shits for people to let their ideals mess up their lives."

Possibly he was older than I thought. "Go on."

"We spent the afternoon working on exhibits. She had some great ideas: alternate mining methods that weren't as environmentally destructive: some *in situ* techniques that probably wouldn't work, but sounded good: even a solar-powered retort, to boil out the oil. Our lawyers were loaded for bear."

"Keep going."

"We knocked off about five. She wanted to take me out to dinner and the way she was, I just wanted to sniff her, so we went down to Larimer Square, poked around in the stores, saw the movie at The Flick, and ate. Then we went home."

"You mean the apartment?"

"Funny. That night, it felt like a home."

"After you took your shower, what did you do?"

"I got that telephone call. The rest you know."

"Tell me about the call."

"There isn't much to tell," he said. "This guy—or it could have been a girl, I guess."

"The voice was disguised?"

"Yes."

"That's something," I said. "He or she apparently knows you." Garver gaped at me. "Go on."

"Whoever it was told me he had the details on a bribe. Said he could prove an EPA official—that's Environmental Protective Agency—was on the take, illegally granting industrial variances to anti-pollution standards. He wanted to know if I was interested in the details."

"And you were?"

36

"Hell, yes. I've suspected it for a long time. He wouldn't give me anything over the phone, though. Said I'd have to meet him at the Blue Bell Bar in Castle Rock in an hour or so, so I said okay, I'd be there."

"Then what?"

"I told JoAnn. At first I thought she was sore about it— me going out on one of our last nights—but then I realized she was nervous. She wanted to come with me, but the voice specifically instructed me to come alone."

"Go on."

"I wasn't even thinking about anything happening to her, but called Carruthers just to make her feel better."

"What time was that?"

"About twenty of ten. 'Gunsmoke' was on and Gene didn't want to come up until ten when it was over, but said he'd come up then. JoAnn made a face at me for calling, but she felt better about it too."

"Did you lock the door when you left?"

"Yes. It was locked when I got back too."

"Then?"

"About ten thirty I got to Castle Rock and started look- ing for the Blue Bell Bar. Castle Rock isn't all that big— maybe a mile of business street, but no more—but I couldn't find it. I thought, some sonuvabitch is really funny. I thought I'd get to work the next day and find something on my desk, like a note from Batman on a Blue Bell Bar match cover from some other town. I finally called the telephone company and they had no listing for a Blue Bell Bar, so I came back."

"Go on."

"Nobody in my apartment. So I went down to Car- ruthers's and he told me what I've already told you." Sud- denly he spun around in his chair so I couldn't see his face. "Why *kill* her? Jesus. Why kill anybody?"

"Do you have any idea who could have done it?"

"No."

"Did anyone threaten her?"

37

"Not that I know of." He wiped his nose and glared at me. "It had to have been a nut. Who else would put her in a waterbed?"

"What about Sharon?"

"You saw her last night. It knocked her so hard she passed out. She isn't strong enough to get her in there, anyway."

I started thinking again about that cool glass of whisky and it made me restless. "She could have had help," I said, getting up.

"Hey. Anything wrong?" Phillip asked, reaching for my arm. "You look pale."

My mind had flashed a picture of Timothy, collapsed in the death chair at Canon City with that stupid grin sloughing off his face. "The arraignment's tomorrow," I said. "See you there."

"You all right?"

"Yes," I said, jerking my arm away from him and banging on the door. I had to get out of there.

5

I tried to focus on the crowd behind me, then gave up. The Judge hadn't come in; neither had Garver; I thought there might be time for a nap. I put my head on the counsel table and shut my eyes.

"Mr. Tree? Don't mean to bother you," someone said, jostling my elbow, "but what's going to happen today?"

By turning my head to one side I could see a yellow pole with a red flag near the top. That couldn't be right. I kept watching until it turned into a young man wearing a tie. "Let go of my elbow," I said.

"Are you all right? Hey. You loaded?"

The question struck me as disrespectful. I pushed myself up and stared into the fellow's face. He wore a mustache and held a notebook in his hand, and had the arrogant look of a reporter. "None of your fucking business, young man," I said. "You can quote me." I put my head down and tried again, but the commotion wouldn't go away. People behind me kept talking and scuffling their feet . . . then a heavy hand closed on my shoulder and started shaking it. "Let go of my shoulder," I said.

"Jesus, Nathan. Wake up."

It sounded like old Charlie Riggs. "Hey," I said, looking up. "It's old Charlie Riggs." I had it in mind to get up but something went wrong, and I kind of lay across the table.

He looked worried about something. "Jesus. If the Judge sees you like this . . ."

I heard a buzzing noise from the counsel table reserved for the prosecution. Somebody's over there, I thought. I looked around Charlie's stomach like an Indian peeking at a wagon train from behind a rock, and found a Face on the other side of the stomach, staring back. "What have you done with my client?" I said first.

Peter Rollander, the DA's chief trial deputy, looked surprised. "I don't . . . Nothing. We haven't done anything."

I thought he'd try to deny it. "Well, where is he then?" I demanded, and waited for an explanation.

Rollander's expression changed. "What the hell is wrong with you, Tree?" He stomped toward one of the doors that leads into the Judge's chambers. "I'm not going through with *this*," I heard him say.

Suddenly Charlie moved and I fell down. When I looked up from the floor a whole ring of faces was frowning down at me. "Hey, Charlie," I said, searching through them for his. "Where are you?"

"Jesus, Nathan. Get up."

I thought it over and decided it wasn't so bad on the floor. "Why? The Judge here?"

Riggs made a sign at Tony the Bailiff, and the two of them gripped me under the arms and pulled me to my feet. I didn't mind. It was almost as comfortable as lying on the floor. "We got to get him out of here," Charlie said.

My feet worked all right but my body seemed to be at an angle. Then it felt as though I might throw up. "I could use a bathroom, boys. Quick."

"Where can we take him, Tony?"

"Division Three," Tony said. "Bowman's on vacation. We can use his can." They took me through the clerk's office and into the hall.

"Mr. Tree?" a nice woman said. "I'm Phillip Garver's mother, and . . . My God, Mr. Tree. What happened?"

"Get me out of here, Charlie."

They pushed me into a bathroom. "Put your finger down your throat, you damn fool," Charlie said.

I did and started retching into the toilet. It occurred to me I was on my ass. "Tony, can you get me some time?"

"Go ahead," Riggs told him. "Maybe he'll be okay."

Somehow I got my clothes off and climbed in the shower. I turned on the cold water and hung on. Finally it began to feel warm and my head started to clear.

"You don't have all day, pal."

A few minutes later we walked back into the courtroom. Charlie stayed close, ready to catch me if I should fall, but I knew what to do because I've done it before. I persuaded myself the world had tipped, and if I was going to stay on it, I'd have to adjust. Then I held myself at the same peculiar angle. Garver sat at the counsel table and grinned, but a distinguished-looking man I vaguely recognized, sitting with Garver's mother, looked far from amused. Up yours, I thought, and sat down.

Tony nodded at the court reporter, who stood by the door to the Judge's chambers, and Rollander marched by me to his table. Then the buzzer sounded and Tony, looking important, rose to his feet. "Everyone please stand," he said. A black-robed man opened the door behind the bench and peered benevolently around the room. "The District Court, City and County of Denver and State of Colorado, the Honorable Orin T. Lester presiding, is now in session," Tony said, pounding his desk with a gavel. "You may be seated."

"Well, now," the Judge said when the scuffling had stopped. "Mr. Tree has arrived, I see, and Mr. Rollander is here." He had short, thick hair and wore glasses, and his customary expression showed tremendous concern for all mankind. "Are both sides ready to proceed?"

I nodded and Rollander said, "Yes, Your Honor."

"This is Case Number 75 CR 8558, the People of the State of Colorado versus Phillip Garver," the Judge said.

41

"Mr. Tree, would you bring your client to the lectern please?"

By keeping my hand on the counsel table and walking slow, I managed it. Garver had to take care of himself.

"Do you have a copy of the information?" Lester asked.

"We do, Judge," I said.

"Do you desire . . ."

"We'll waive a reading of it. Wait." I tried to read it and then handed it to Garver. "Does it say JoAnn White, or Cora Shannon?" I whispered.

"JoAnn White."

"Your Honor, the information should be amended to reflect the true name of the deceased," I said. "They've got it wrong. It's Cora Shannon, not JoAnn White."

Rollander jumped up and then uncertainly started to sit down. "Mr. Rollander?" Lester asked. "Can you shed some light on the subject? Mr. Tree, it appears, doesn't think you've correctly designated the victim."

"JoAnn White was the victim's alias, Judge," I said. "She worked for an oil . . ."

"Just a moment. I object, Your Honor. Mr. Tree's remarks are probably self-serving. I object most strenuously."

"Mr. Tree?"

"Well, if the DA wants to prove my client murdered someone who never existed, I guess that'll be all right."

There was laughter in the courtroom, which surprised me. I hadn't meant to be funny. "Order!" Lester commanded, banging the bench with his gavel. It quieted down. "Mr. Rollander, I suggest you investigate the matter of the name of the deceased. If it develops Mr. Tree is correct, then perhaps the information can be amended *ex parte*. Will that be all right with you, Mr. Tree?"

"Fine."

"Very well." The Judge looked at Garver. "Are you Phillip Garver?" he asked.

"Yes sir."

"How do you plead to the information—and to the information as it may be amended—on file against you? Guilty or not guilty?"

"Not guilty."

"The Clerk will note the accused has entered a plea of 'Not guilty.' Mr. Tree, do you wish a preliminary hearing in this matter?"

"What?" My mind had wandered off, and I tried to bring it back.

"I said, do you wish a preliminary hearing?"

"Yes."

"Very well. This is Monday, July thirteenth. How much time do you need, Mr. Rollander, to prepare for the preliminary?"

"Two weeks, if it please the Court. I've already had one surprise, and . . ."

"Two weeks?" I asked. "What about bail, then?"

"Frankly, Mr. Tree, the Court is not disposed to set bail," Lester said. "The charge is first-degree murder and the facts appear rather bizarre. I suggest you bring up the matter of bail at the preliminary if you feel you can wait that long."

My tongue felt like a piece of watermelon. "I don't follow that," I said, trying to say what it was I was thinking. "So what if the facts are bizarre? That doesn't mean anything as far as guilt or innocence, does it? All it means is the facts are bizarre."

Lester's jaw got stiff. "I believe you're entitled to have the matter of bail considered, Mr. Tree, and I've considered it. Now as to the prelim—"

"I believe I'm entitled to have it set, Judge. I respectfully ask you to set it."

"Very well. Two hundred thousand dollars, cash bond." He appeared satisfied with himself. "That is a record in this court, Mr. Tree, in case you're interested."

"A two hundred thousand dollar cash bond will cost my client twenty thousand dollars, Judge."

43

"Are you worried about your fee, sir?" Lester asked. There was laughter in the courtroom again, but the Judge let it roll on before calling for order.

"Move to reduce bail, Judge," I said.

"I'll oppose the motion, Your Honor," Rollander said. "In fact, I don't think it's high enough."

"Very well. In view of the opposition of Mr. Rollander to your motion, Mr. Tree, I'll have to set it down for hearing." He consulted his calendar and shook his head with sadness. "I'm afraid the soonest I can hear it is two weeks from today," he said. "That will be Monday, July twenty-seventh, at ten A.M. Immediately after your motion, we can have the preliminary hearing."

"That's the best you can do?" I asked.

"Yes it is."

"It will suit me quite well, Your Honor," Rollander said.

"Very well. So ordered," Lester said. He started to get up. "The defendant is remanded to the custody of the Sheriff. Is there anything further, gentlemen?"

Rollander glared at me as though I was getting away with something. "Your Honor, I think the record should reflect . . ." Then he changed his mind. "Should reflect that Mr. Garver is represented by Nathan Tree."

"I'm sure the reporter got the names. Anything else?"

"No sir."

"Very well. Court will be in recess."

My hackles were up and, besides, I never had liked Rollander. Not only did he sport a mustache but he was also tall and young and wore silk suits. "What did you want in the record, Rollander?" I asked when the Judge had gone. "Something about my condition?"

"Just what is obvious, Mr. Tree. No more than that." He gathered up his books and walked out.

I sweated my way up the steps of the old West Side Court Building, which squatted on an island surrounded by asphalt streets in what used to be an old part of town. The old building was made of red sandstone bricks the size of boulders, but looked out of place in the new Denver, like a wilderness fort in a subdivision. At one time it was large enough to hold all the divisions of the Denver District Court, the Sheriff's office, the DA's office, and the jail. Now the building was too small for the DA.

I walked into the high-ceilinged lobby. "Mr. Rollander in?" I asked an aging receptionist, whose heavy body and neuter appearance seemed to have taken on the aspect of the building.

"Why, Mr. Tree, remember me? I'm Ada Little!"

I looked at her closely and then remembered a well-groomed woman of forty who joined the staff just before I resigned. She used to hate herself for eating doughnuts. "Sure enough. How are you, Ada?" I said. "You've gained some weight, but I always thought you were too thin anyway."

"Oh, Mr. Tree, you'll never get to heaven telling whoppers like that!" We talked a few minutes as though we'd been old friends, which we hadn't been, and then she told me which door to knock on.

Rollander's office had a high ceiling, thick red carpet, and aging wallpaper that had been painted yellow. At one time the space had been the chambers for a judge, and the heavy wooden furniture still echoed that slower day. When I walked in Rollander stood up, but didn't offer his hand. "Have a chair, Mr. Tree," he said, then jerked the telephone off his desk and barked a few commands at his secretary. Then he crouched on his chair like an executive with too much to do. "Now. What can I do for you?"

"I could use a cup of coffee."

He snorted and jerked the phone off its hook again. A moment later his secretary appeared with one cup of coffee, which she handed to me and quickly left.

"Have you verified the name of that unfortunate girl who zippered herself up in that waterbed?" I asked.

He didn't even smile. "We're working on it."

"She was a petroleum geologist for Dolores Petroleum.

45

William Drake, the president of the company, should . . ."

"He already has. We're locating next of kin now."

"I got you pretty good on that one," I said, testing.

"It'll even out." He stared without expression over the top of my head. "We never thought to question her identity and the people we interviewed said there was no family."

"Who told you that?"

"A Ms. Barney Madden. She works for Garver and seemed to know the deceased quite well."

"Why don't you drop the charges against Garver, Peter?" I said, taking some coffee. "This was obviously an oil company conspiracy of some kind. Everybody knows how ruthless they are." He looked bored. "The poor girl got in the way somehow," I said.

"An interesting theory."

"It could use a few details, but I expect it'll work."

The young man didn't respond to my charm. "There are other ways to look at it, of course," he finally said. "Garver found out she was an oil company spy, so he strangled her."

"That's only the way it looks, Peter. You know nothing is the way it looks." He tapped his fingers on his desk, waiting. "What's the evidence on Garver?" I asked.

"You'll have to be more specific, Mr. Tree."

"All right. Do you have an autopsy report?"

He opened the pedestal to his desk and pulled out a file, which I reached for. "Oh no," he said, evading my hand. "I can't let you see it. We don't operate that way now."

"Lord."

"I'll discuss it with you if you'd like."

"Just read it to me."

"The time of death can't be fixed with exactitude," he said, scanning the report. "She was sealed in an airtight environment that prevented normal decay of bodily tissue. However, bacterial expansion indicates she'd been dead from five to ten days."

"She disappeared Monday night, didn't she?"

"That's our information."

"Anything to suggest she was not murdered Monday night?"

"No. But it could have been a couple of days on either side."

"What about cause of death?"

"Apparently, strangulation."

"What do you mean 'apparently'? Isn't the pathologist certain?"

"I can't comment on his degree of certainty, Mr. Tree. You can ask him that yourself when he's on the stand."

I began staring at Rollander's mustache, thinking I might get it to twitch. "When you say 'strangulation,' do you mean she was drowned, or strangled?"

"Strangled."

"No water in her lungs?"

"That's right."

"So she was dead before she was sealed in the waterbed?"

"Anything the report might say on that subject would be conjecture, Mr. Tree. I won't bother you with it."

"What about criminal agency?" I asked, still staring.

"As I've already stated, it says she was strangled."

"By what? A piece of bread down the wrong tube?"

The right side of his mustache began to work, which was good to know. At the trial I might get it going hard enough to close his eye. "Nothing in here about food strangulation," he said. "However, there is factual data to support an inference that hands were placed around her throat and that her trachea was manually squeezed, shutting off oxygen and resulting in death."

"What is that data?"

"Bruises on her throat and neck, consistent with the placement of fingers."

"From the front or the back?"

"The back."

"Any other bruises on her body? Anything to suggest a struggle?"

"She had a small bruise on her left thigh and one on her right bicep."

"That's all?"

"That's all he mentions in his report."

"Anything under her fingernails?"

"Good point," he said, as though proud of me. He made a note in the margin. "No mention of anything like that."

"What's the date of the report?"

"Yesterday. Sunday, July twelfth."

"Who's the pathologist?"

"Dr. Julius A. Belden."

I fished around for a piece of paper and made a few notes.

"Was she conscious or unconscious when the factual data occurred that could support an inference that hands were placed around her throat?"

"What?"

"Conscious or unconscious when she was strangled?"

The tip of his mustache almost hit him in the eye. That worked so well that I considered offering him a Rolaid to get him thinking about his stomach, but decided to save it for the trial. "No mention one way or the other."

"You don't suppose she just stood there while he strangled her?"

"I never 'suppose' anything."

"Aren't you curious? No evidence of a struggle except a couple of bruises anyone could have, and nothing to show she was unconscious when it happened?" He said nothing. "Here we have a killing, ladies and gentlemen," I said, "where the victim stood quietly by while her boy friend in a terrible rage choked her to death."

"It's possible the report doesn't go far enough."

"You aren't planning on burying that one and getting another one, are you?"

He controlled himself with great effort. "It's possible

48

Belden missed a few points. I certainly intend to find out."

I leaned back in the chair and scratched my stomach. "As I remember, the prosecution has a duty to disclose information the defense can't reasonably be expected to get on its own, such as autopsy reports. How come you're being such a horse's ass about this, Peter?"

He rose to his feet. "Your insults are something I don't have to take, Tree. Get out."

The performance struck me as staged. "Are you hiding something?"

"Get the hell out of here."

"No," I said, "you'll have to throw me out, which will lay a better foundation for my motion." He hesitated. "If I'm forced to leave, I'll be back with a court reporter so our dialogue can be a part of the motion."

He sat down and glared at his watch. I tried to figure it out. "Any evidence of sexual molestation?"

"No. None."

"Was she pregnant?"

He took a deep breath. "Yes. Less than a month."

"Is that it?"

"Is that what, Mr. Tree?"

I suddenly realized this youngster was not going to be easy. The pregnancy of Garver's earthmate-oil-company-spy couldn't be kept secret for long. The press might have it already. Was he dragging a skunk across the track? "The autopsy says she was strangled from the back, was pregnant, and had been dead between five and ten days. What else does it say?"

"Please be specific, Mr. Tree." He looked at his watch again. "Incidentally, I have a hearing at . . ."

"Was Garver's apartment searched?"

"Yes."

"What was taken out of it?"

He pulled another file out of the pedestal of his desk. "A knife. Presumably the one used to cut the mattress, be-

49

cause bits of the material the mattress is made of were on it."

"Can you describe it?"

"Wooden-handled kitchen knife with bread slicing teeth."

"Any fingerprints?"

"Yes. Yours."

"Mine?"

"Clever, Tree. I can't think of a more innocent-seeming way to cover the prints of your client."

"What else was taken?"

"The victim's personal effects and the repair kit for the waterbed."

"Had it been used recently?"

"We believe it was used to patch the mattress after Garver put in the girl. It has a roll of multivinyl chloride forty-two inches long. The cut at the end of the roll matches one of the ends on the roll used to patch the waterbed."

"Fingerprints on the repair kit or anything in it?"

"No."

I was running out of questions and still hadn't hit it. Rollander stood up. "Mr. Tree . . ."

"Did you find anything that might suggest someone other than Garver was there the night she was killed?"

"Specifically, who?"

I thought his mustache moved. "Anyone other than the girl or Garver."

"Of course," he said. "Your fingerprints on the knife, for example. Probably you picked up the knife Saturday night at his party, but we don't know."

"I'm talking about Monday night."

"How could we know . . ." He stopped talking.

"You found something, Rollander. I want to know what it is."

"File a motion."

"If I do, you can be sure every reporter in town will be there, and I'll raise every question I can."

His mustache twitched even though the line of his mouth didn't move. "We found a fingerprint on the shelf near the repair kit."

"Whose?"

"The man's name was Watt Chambers."

I tried to remember where I'd heard the name, then remembered the argument with the Robinson girl at Garver's party. "That black man who was murdered Monday night?"

"Yes."

I got up, trying to understand it. "Where was the print?"

"On a shelf in a closet in Garver's bedroom. Near the repair kit."

"How do you account for it?"

"Garver and Chambers knew each other. Chambers obviously was in the apartment some time other than the night the girl was murdered."

"Can you prove that?"

"I don't have to. That print has nothing to do with the case. But I can tell you we're prepared to rebut any inference you might try to draw from it."

"Nothing to do with the case? A fingerprint found near the repair kit used to seal up the girl, of a man who was murdered on the same night the girl was murdered, and you say nothing to do with the case?"

"Denver's a big city now, Mr. Tree. There were two other homicides that night. Were they connected too?" He allowed himself a smile. "Furthermore, Chambers was executed by a black militant group. And as far as the time of the girl's death, it might not have been the same night at all."

"Is the police department considering the possibility of a connection between the murders?"

"It's their investigation, Mr. Tree. We don't interfere."

51

"Will you ask them to let me see their files?"

"No."

"This isn't a game, Rollander. A man—possibly a good man, in spite of his politics—has been accused of murder."

His mustache was as steady as his heavy wooden desk. "I'm aware it isn't a game, Mr. Tree. And it won't become one, either. According to the rules of the game *you* want to play, I'm supposed to provide you with every bit of information from our investigations so you can take advantage of some irrelevant fact that will give you a sporting chance. 'Reasonable doubt.' Get a guilty man off. Isn't that the game?"

"Lord."

"I hear you were real tough, Mr. Tree. Even vindictive. How many men did you convict?"

"I didn't keep score."

"Well, Garver is guilty. He murdered that girl in cold blood, just as sure as—as that Pettersenn fellow you prosecuted blew up his mother." I tried to move but nothing worked. "Pettersenn paid. You saw to that. And Garver will pay too, Mr. Tree. *I'll* see to that."

6

It felt as though my lungs were being smashed. I sat on the steps of the old court house and held my sides, as though trying to cover up a hole. Lord. Finally it got better, and I got in my truck and drove toward the Oilmen Club Building.

The huge, new building is one of the blessings of Urban Renewal. I remembered how hard I had fought, fifteen years ago, to keep the government from using taxpayers' money to flatten the old town and put skyscrapers where it had been. I was convinced the project foreshadowed the end of our civilization, which was the way my father had felt about Social Security, and his father had felt about the income tax. They are dead now, I thought, and "what happens next" is not one of my concerns. But we were right, I thought, searching for a place to park. It's just taken America longer to crumble than any of us expected.

Great Mesa Shale had a suite on the fifth floor and Dolores Petroleum was on the nineteenth. I tried Dolores Petroleum first.

William Drake bustled into the reception room immediately after I was announced. "Mr. Tree? Gee! This is awful!" He had a young, unlined face and brilliant white teeth, but his large body sagged with too much fat. He led me down a hallway to his office: executive size, on a corner of the building, with huge windows on two sides. The view of the mountains was spectacular and we seemed to be drifting their way.

"Like some coffee? Sit down, please. Boy, am I glad you came by. I've been talking to policemen all day, but you can't get anything *out* of them!" He spoke with the urgency of an adolescent. "Zelda? Two coffees, hon," he said into a speaker. "Did you say black?"

"Yes."

"What has *happened?*" he said, focusing on me. "I can't believe it. Cora was just a super person, and now she's *dead*."

"Do you have any idea who killed her?"

"That sonuvabitch Garver. He may be your client, but to me he's a sonuvabitch."

"I thought you two young stallions hit it off."

"Hit it off?" He had started to light a pipe. "I don't even know him." He got the pipe going and blew out the match. Zelda brought the coffee and set the cups on his desk. She smiled at me—a young smile in a firm, tanned face—and I was glad for the interruption. "Your name is William Drake, isn't it?"

"Of course it is." He looked puzzled.

"Cora Shannon was a petroleum geologist, employed by your company?"

"Sure."

"I'm confused. Garver told me he met you two months ago."

"I'd remember it, Mr. Tree. I sure don't remember it. Where?"

"Here. With Cora."

"That's not so. She took off for Europe three months ago —at least that's what *I* thought—and I haven't seen her since."

"Did she quit?"

"No. But she'd been working hard—real hard—and

54

wanted some time, and it fit in with our plans so I let her go. We called it a sabbatical so we could pay her something and write it off."

"You say you thought she was in Europe?"

"Yes."

"Then you didn't know she was living with Garver?"

The color in his face deepened and he bit the stem of his pipe. "I don't believe that. She wouldn't do that."

"I take it the police told you?"

"Yes." He swirled the coffee in his cup, staring at it moodily. "Was it true?"

"That's right. She used the name 'JoAnn White.'"

He spun around in his chair, jumped to his feet, and glared out the window. "That sonuvabitch."

"How long did she work for you?"

"Two years."

"Didn't she do a lot of work on that Great Mesa land?"

"Where'd you hear about that?" he asked.

"Dolores Petroleum wanted to buy it and she did a survey to see what it was worth?"

"That's extremely confidential information, Mr. Tree. I'd like to know your source."

"And the lawsuit between Clear Sky and Great Mesa was one you wanted Clear Sky to win, right? In the hope Dix would get discouraged and sell out?"

He dropped in his chair and stared at me as though I had magical power. "Where did you hear all this?"

"Garver. He told me he met you two months ago and you explained it all to him."

"It isn't true. I mean, sure, we wanted Clear Sky to win and we wanted to buy their land, but . . . Oh, God." His voice seemed to have caught on something. He got up again and wandered toward the window. "She knew how much we needed that land. I wonder if maybe . . . you know."

"What's it worth?"

"He's got four sections in the Piceance Basin, which is

55

about twenty-five hundred acres. The stuff isn't as good as he thinks—about thirty-five gallons of oil to a ton of rock—but it's easy to get to and we think we can treat the spent shale and sell it as fertilizer."

"In terms of dollars, what's it worth?"

"Fifty million. We'll go to sixty."

"I can remember when you could get all you wanted of that land for five dollars an acre. Now you tell me you'll pay sixty million dollars for four sections?"

"There are four hundred million barrels of oil in there. If we can buy it for ten to twelve cents a barrel, we want it."

"What does Dix think it's worth?"

"About twice that. He thinks it'll run seventy to eighty gallons to the ton, that he's got more than a billion barrels." He put another match to his pipe. "He doesn't have that much. Cora's maps and reports prove it."

"Are you still trying to buy it?"

"Yes. I talked to him yesterday."

"What are your chances?"

"Good. He wants out. He's had it."

I got up. "You're sure you've never met Garver?"

"No. If I ever do, I'll kill him."

You aren't the type, I thought, and left.

The offices of Great Mesa Shale were old-fashioned, compared to Dolores Petroleum. They were cluttered with wooden tables and work benches over which high-intensity lamps hung, like vultures clamped to branches; and surface and sub-surface contour maps were hanging from the walls. An elderly woman with spectacles hanging from a chain pinned to her shirt watched me come in the door, then continued typing at a leisurely pace on a manual machine. A gleaming electric typewriter stood unused on a file cabinet. She finished a line, carefully marked her place, and found me again. "Yes."

"Is Mr. Dix here?"

"He left early, poor dear. I don't expect him back."

"Will he be in tomorrow?"

"I really don't know, but you're welcome to try."

A framed photographic portrait hung on the wall behind the woman's desk. A grim-looking man with a contrived smile gazed powerfully into the room. "Is that him?" I asked, pointing.

"Yes. Ten years ago. He looks just the same today, except . . ."

"Go on."

"You're Nathan Tree, aren't you?"

"That's right."

"I've seen your picture, Mr. Tree. At one time Mr. Dix was a great admirer of yours." She pushed at her hair. "I'm sure he'd like to talk to you. Is it about Phillip Garver?"

"Yes."

"Can you come back tomorrow around two?"

"Thank you, Miss . . . ?"

"I'm Mrs. Dix, Mr. Tree. Pleased to meet you."

When I got back to my office, I called Joe Reddman. I didn't want to: the only way to be certain a thing will get done right is to do it yourself; but, in spite of that, I knew I had to have help.

At one time Joe was an All-American halfback, but gave up football for handball, cops, and robbers. There's no doubt in my mind that he's the best investigator in the state—including Charlie Riggs—but he's also more mule-headed than the average jackass, and getting him to work requires a finesse I am not always able to demonstrate. "Joe? Nathan Tree," I said when I had him on the line.

"Mmm."

"You busy?"

"Yes."

"Joe, I've stumbled into the . . ."

"That waterbed thing in the paper."

57

"Yes. I wish to hell I hadn't gotten into it, but I've got to admit I'm fascinated by it. The damnedest . . ."

"No, Nathan," he said. "Not my style."

" 'Style!' What the hell are you talking about?" I asked, even though I knew what he meant. The "Waterbed Murder," as it had been dubbed by the press, had the look of a puzzle, and Joe was more physical than that. "Look. My client has a lot of money. Anything you want, within reason." There was no reply. "You might even get your picture in the paper."

"What I need," he said. "Riches and fame."

I don't pretend to understand the man. Most of the people who know him call him "the Last Wild Indian," and without knowing what that means, I have the feeling it's true. "Damn it Reddman, the man is innocent. Does that mean anything to you? I need help!"

"Then get what you need," he said.

"What do you mean?"

"An agency, Nathan. Not one man. An outfit that can give you background checks, probably twenty-four hour surveillance on some people, fast answers to intriguing questions. I can't do all that."

He was right, of course. That's one of the things I don't like about the man. "Who can I call?"

"Try the Rocky Mountain Bureau of Investigation," he said.

"The *who?* For Christ sake, Joe. They sound like PR men."

"Yeah. They are. But the Policemen's Union hired them, so at least they can tell you what the cops have."

I called them up and a few minutes later drove over. Their office was on Acoma Street near the new court house, in a low, flat-roofed building I remembered from days gone by. It once belonged to a bail bondsman I'd prosecuted for extortion, and after that it was a pawn shop. The building was yellow then instead of an official-

58

looking green, and there was no gold shield painted on the plate-glass window facing the sidewalk.

A girl with piled-up blond hair and large breasts sat behind a small wooden desk, writing a letter. When she saw me she pasted the wad of gum she'd been chewing against the roof of her mouth and turned the page over. "Hello. May I help you?"

I asked for Richard Hunter, the "Agent in Charge of Investigations," and told her who I was.

"*You're* Mr. Tree?" she asked, then blushed and got to her feet. She was dressed in the kind of skirt cheerleaders used to wear—they probably don't wear anything now—and her long, muscular legs were all I could see. I cleared my throat. "Won't you be seated, Mr. Tree? I'll tell him you're here."

The small carpeted room had been paneled with mahogany-stained plasterboard, and I sat on an office couch under the window. When she returned, she said, "He'll be right out, Mr. Tree," and busied herself with important-looking papers.

Two or three minutes later—apparently what was judged to be a decent interval—the door reopened and a young man wearing a turtleneck shirt and smoking a pipe strode into the room. He had black hair, the thoughtful expression of a scientist searching for meaning, and the heavily muscled body of a weight lifter. "Mr. Tree?"

"That's right."

"I'm Richard Hunter. Come in."

I followed him into a small, clean, paneled room with a rug on the floor, an austere-looking metal desk toward the back, and two chairs. There was nothing on the desk and no pictures on the walls. It looked like the executive office of a political fanatic. "Everything you say will be recorded on our recorder system, Mr. Tree. Standard Operating Procedure."

"Lord."

"What?"

"Nothing."

He perched on the desk and smiled, studying me as I sat down. "Want me to turn it off?"

"Suit yourself."

"I've heard a lot about you, Mr. Tree. Even before this waterbed murder." His eyes continued their investigation. "That's what you want to talk about, I hope."

"Yes."

"Don't mind telling you we'd be delighted to get it. We're just starting in this town, case like that would be a real boost. Most of us are from the East and we have ideas the agencies here never heard of. We're tough, modern, experienced—every person on my staff has at least three years of investigative work—and I don't mind telling you, we're the best."

I fought down the impulse to get up and walk out. The Easterners were taking over the town, I thought, and no matter that my grandparents had done the same thing to the Indians. But I settled back and listened, which he expected me to do, as he explained techniques, procedures, and charges. Then he asked me what I had in mind.

"Some backgrounds to start with," I said. "Tomorrow or the next day I'll want a lady followed."

The small, calculating smile of a salesman who has closed a deal blew across his face. A legal pad and ball-point pen appeared in his hand. "Let's start with the backgrounds. Okay?"

"All right. Cora Shannon, also known as JoAnn White. Everything you can get: education, family, previous jobs and performance. Also whether she was on a sabbatical from Dolores Petroleum when she was killed. Find out too if anyone at the Clear Sky office knew who she really was."

He grinned. "Good thing that recorder system is on," he said, I suppose to justify the expense. "Next?"

"William Drake and the Dolores Petroleum Company. Focus on anything irregular. Find out if anything was

60

going on between the Shannon girl and Drake. Anything romantic."

"Fine."

"Robert Dix and Great Mesa Shale, also anything strange. He's a crusty old bastard—don't waste time on personality quirks, except if they're relevant—but go deep."

"Gotcha."

"Eugene Carruthers. He lives in the Gates Tower and is a psychologist of some sort. Not an interview, by the way, on any of these people. I'll do that. I don't want them to know you're looking into their backgrounds."

"Low profile, you mean?"

"I expect that's what I mean. On Watt Chambers . . ."

"The black guy, killed about a week ago?"

"His fingerprints were in Garver's apartment. Find out if the police think there was a connection."

Hunter's expression registered pleasure. "You want to put it on Chambers? Beautiful! Black militant—probably violence in his past—ought to get good mileage . . ."

"Not a background," I said. "Just find out what the police have, if you can."

"Easy. Anyone else?"

"Sharon Garver and her husband Pete. Backgrounds."

"They related to Phillip?" Hunter asked.

"Brother and sister-in-law. She's the one I'll want followed, too. By people who can stay out of sight but can spot trouble and move in if they have to."

He tapped the pen against his teeth. "If we need to be ready for trouble, Mr. Tree, it'd help if we knew why you want her followed."

I'd been thinking about Sharon. "She may be next," I said. "Until I know what she knows, I can't afford to lose her."

He grinned at me, as though to say, "Beautiful."

7

I got out of bed the next morning and glanced out the window. The air was clean and the brick building and tree-lined parkway across the street stood against the sky with brilliant clarity. I had forgotten how pretty Denver can be. The background noise of motors and wheels hadn't started its incessant clang and you could hear and see the squirrels and birds, whose quick moves jiggled the scene with little splashes of life.

I dressed and went outside. It had been a late spring and there were still patches of snow on Mount Evans, and from Denver, with the sunlight hitting them, they looked like smiles. The snow had lead in it, of course—a byproduct of so many cars spewing exhaust into Colorado's rarefied air—and the lead poisoned the wildlife, but that was all right. The important thing nowadays is the view. I climbed in my truck and drove toward the county jail.

The visitors' rooms at the county jail are identical to the ones in the police building, and Garver grinned when he saw me. "How's your head?"

"It's on."

"That was some load you carried into court yesterday. I was impressed." The inane grin remained plastered to his face. "Maybe some day you'll give me a chance to see if I can keep up."

"I drink alone," I said.

"Jesus. Sorry."

"I talked to the DA yesterday."

"And?"

I told him, starting with the autopsy, then asked him if he'd known JoAnn was pregnant. His face had turned gray. "Damn her," he said. "God damn her."

His reaction startled me. He had hunched over the table as though it was a canoe that had turned over, and he was hanging on for dear life. "Snap out of it, Phillip. What the hell are you talking about?"

"I lied when I told you it wasn't a big deal between us. It was a very big deal to me. Just not to her."

"Go on."

"About a month ago we had this real heavy scene." His red eyes burned at mine. "I'd asked her to marry me— damnedest thing, it just slid out, but I meant it—and she said, 'Oh no. None of that mama–papa bullshit for me.'" He choked out a laugh. "Then she told me she wanted my child. Never met a man whose baby she wanted, she said. The experience of being a woman, or some damn thing—a girl if she was lucky, but if it was a boy, she wanted him to look like me—Jesus. Corny as hell. What a scene."

"What did you tell her?"

"I said no. Not a question of support: she was independent as all hell, had a good career and all that. But if she wanted my baby she could by god marry me and we'd have a dozen, and the hell with ecology. I even made her promise she'd keep taking the pill."

"Well—dry your tears," I said. I'd intended to say something sympathetic, but that's what came out. "Drake says he never met you."

"That's a lie. We talked at least an hour."

"You're sure it was Drake?"

63

"I didn't take his fingerprints, but it was in the Dolores Petroleum office and JoAnn told me that's who it was."

"What did he look like?"

"Real white teeth. Good-looking guy—deep tan—heavy body. Tall."

"Anyone see you?"

"No. JoAnn even wore a wig. Said she had to because otherwise it might get back to Dix."

"What about a secretary or a janitor?"

"This was about six o'clock. The only one around was Drake."

It struck me as too neat. "Didn't you call him last week to see if he'd heard from the Shannon girl?"

"Yes."

"What did he say?"

"I never got past his secretary."

I happened to look at the back of my hands and saw how the skin had started to wrinkle. What the hell am I doing in town? "How well did you know Watt Chambers?"

"The black guy who got shot last week?"

"Yes."

"I didn't know him at all. Why?"

"You'd never met him?"

"No. Yes. I did too. A few months ago."

"Are you being evasive?"

"No. I'm trying to remember." He stared out the bar-slatted window. "I was the chairman of a committee—Better Schools for Greater Denver—and we were trying to elect school board members who would support busing as a means to achieve integrated schools. Chambers was on the committee."

"Was he ever in your apartment?"

"I think so. The committee met there twice."

"Do you have an impression of him?"

"Quiet. Seemed like a nice guy. A helluva painter, I heard."

64

"His fingerprints were found in the closet where you kept the repair kit."

"What? How'd they get there?"

"Those meetings in your apartment: Did you show off your waterbed or the repair kit?"

"No."

"Did Chambers go into your bedroom alone? To use the bathroom?"

"He might have. He wasn't a creep, though. I don't see him prowling through my closet."

"Who can I talk to about him?"

He thought a moment. "Try Georgia Robinson. I heard they lived together."

"That name is familiar. Do I know her?"

"Come on, Nathan. She's that leggy young thing at my party you kept staring at."

"But she's . . ."

"White." He shook his head at me. "You really are kind of an old bastard."

I got up and paced the floor. "I've hired a detective agency. You'll be paying for it, so you should know about it."

"How come?"

"Primarily to have your sister-in-law followed."

"Why do that?"

"She knows something. I want to find out what it is."

"I don't believe you."

"Oh? You've given lots of parties, haven't you?" He nodded. "Ever had one where a whole group of people stood around on your waterbed?"

"No, but it doesn't surprise me. Once a bunch of outlaws started playing strip poker in the elevator."

"Still, this is the first time the guests wound up barefoot on the waterbed, isn't it?"

"That's right."

"And out of all the times it could have happened, this time there was a body in there?" He frowned. "Add to that the way it happened. Sharon brought the subject up, then made the bet, then got everyone to take off their shoes—possibly to protect the mattress, but possibly also to feel the body on the inside."

"No, man! If she'd known she wouldn't have passed out."

"Don't shout, Phillip. I can hear you."

"Damn it, she's not a killer. She couldn't do it."

I stared out the window and into another prison courtyard. It looked as lonely as an iceberg. "Even you could be right," I said. "And I agree with you. There aren't many people who can deliberately kill, and I doubt if she's one of them."

"Then why have her followed?"

"Suppose she knew something was in there, but didn't know what it was. Then it turned out to be a body."

"Jesus."

"She knows something. If she's followed, she might lead us to some answers."

"Can't you just ask her what you want to know?"

"I intend to, but it won't do any good. She hasn't said anything yet, and the longer she waits the more time she'll have to convince herself she can't." Phillip's mouth set into a thin line. "It could also save her life."

"What? Following her? How?"

"Whoever murdered Cora Shannon is one of the 'fortunates' with the ability to kill. If Sharon knows something, how long do you think it'll take him to realize her presence on this earth is a threat?"

He took some deep breaths, as though there wasn't enough oxygen in the air. "Okay," he finally said. "Don't send the bill to me, though. Send it to Dad."

There was no wind that morning and the air had filled with the fumes from a million cars. I drove back to town and parked by the Denver *Chronicle*. The town has turned into a cesspool, I thought, which is another byproduct of

Urban Renewal. As I walked toward the building my face oozed oil, and it gave me a perverse satisfaction to consider again that my grandfather, father, and I had been right.

After waiting a few minutes in the library of the newspaper, a clerk brought me a thick envelope jammed with clippings on Watt Chambers. Some of them dated back seven years and I read through them all. He may have been "a helluva painter" to his friends, but he was something else to the police. In his abbreviated tour of this earth he'd been charged with burglary, rape, and assault, and had been convicted of inciting to riot.

I picked through the reports of his murder, trying to sort the factual from the flights of fancy. Most of the copy was speculation on why he'd been executed by his brethren, but probably through inadvertence at least the essential facts were there. His body had been found in the early morning, just a week ago, in his car on a deserted downtown street. He'd been shot in the head. The weapon, a small-caliber pistol, was in the front part of the car between the door and the seat. A ballistics test proved conclusively it was the death weapon and the police theorized his killer had dropped it right after the shooting.

A note was found next to the body that said, "Death to the Infidel." According to official sources—which probably meant a cop, standing near a reporter—the murder had all the earmarks of an execution. The theory was buttressed by the fact that Chambers was known to have been involved in a power struggle in a violence-prone black militant group, and was generally regarded as a heretic. The article went on to compare Chambers's death with other militant executions, such as the killing of Alex Rackley in New Haven some years before. The reporter was obviously proud of the comparison, I thought, because it seemed to show how Denver had matured.

I stuffed the clippings back in the envelope and got up. Another revolutionary, a malcontent who pretended soci-

67

ety had warped his soul, as an excuse to vent criminal tendencies. But the problem was I no longer quite believed it. There might even have been more to Chambers than my impression of him.

Pete and Sharon Garver lived in an older section of town, in a neighborhood that had been restored by young Liberals. Their mission had been to Save the Inner City, and they succeeded in creating a nice little island. The Garver house was an old two-story brick building with gables and a sharply sloped roof. Three tall spruce trees stood in the lawn like soldiers, guarding it from attack, and the house seemed to crouch in their shadow, as though eavesdropping on the street. Unlike some others on the block, this one was not a cheerful place.

I shut the door to my truck and glanced across the street. Richard Hunter seemed to be sleeping in an old Buick that was parked in the shade of a maple tree. I walked past the spruce trees and onto a narrow wooden porch, where I knocked on the screen door.

"I'll get it, Mommy!"

A serious youngster with freckles, red hair, and four eyes appeared in the foyer and pressed his nose against the screen.

"What's your name, young man?"

"Peter Garver Junior."

"I'm Nathan Tree, Peter. Is your mother here?"

Abruptly he disappeared and a moment later Sharon bustled out of the shadow. "Nathan. What a surprise. Come in!" She opened the door. "Run along, Petey," she said, trying to pry the youngster away from her leg.

"Don't want to."

"Petey! Off you go!" she said, pushing him outside.

"Nothing to do."

Once inside I could see her better. A flame-colored house coat, tied at the waist with a black rope, accented her metallic breasts; but she couldn't seem to meet my eyes and there was something hysterical about her

68

manner. "I can't believe this is happening," she said, leading me into her living room. "It's so *awful*." She waved me into a leather chair. "I suppose it's just another case to you, but to me it's so terribly unreal."

I grunted something intended to sound sympathetic, and sat down opposite a carefully paneled wall that held beautifully polished wooden shelves and cabinets. I can recognize good workmanship, and this was superb. "Did your husband build these?"

Her short laugh cracked like ice. "Hardly. Pete has ten thumbs." She sat down beside them. "They're lovely, aren't they?" she said, leaning toward the dark polished wood of a cabinet door and touching it with her long fingers. She might have been stroking a horse. "Without them I'd never have bought this house."

"Have you lived here long?"

"Four years, ten months, and eighteen days." She spoke with all the sweetness of a nun, praying in church, then lit a cigarette. "You must think I'm terrible. We lived in San Francisco right after we were married though, and everything was so simple there, really. No family dinners to contend with, or family image to live up to. I wish we'd never left."

"Your husband's a teacher, isn't he?"

She nodded. "History, at Denver University. How could they refuse?"

"What do you mean?"

Her face registered distress, as though she would rather not have to say. "His father has been, shall we say, generous in his gifts to the school?"

Someone ought to kick your witch's ass, I thought. "Are we alone?" I asked.

Smoke misted out of her mouth and her voice grew throaty and low. "We could be. What do you have in mind?"

It surprised me. "Are you making a pass at me, young lady?"

"You don't have to be angry."

"Very hospitable of you. Makes me feel like one of the family."

Her manner changed. "I'm really very tired, Nathan," she said, jerking the cigarette in and out of her mouth and crossing her arms in front of her. "If I don't get some rest . . ."

"All right. You passed out Saturday night, and I'm curious about it. Before fainting, did you know what was in the waterbed?"

"I think so. Someone said, 'It feels like a corpse'—and then, that terrible shadow."

"I mean before that."

"Of course not. How could . . . You don't think *I* put her in there?"

"Can you tell me anything about her?"

"Not really. Except everyone seemed so impressed with her, but she didn't fool me. It doesn't surprise me at all that she worked for an oil company."

"You didn't know that?"

"None of us did. Not even Barney."

"Who?"

"Barney Madden. The office manager at Clear Sky."

"When she moved in with Phillip, did that surprise you?"

She snapped out her cigarette. "No."

"Bother you a little?"

"I don't know what you're talking about."

"Phillip tells me it was the best year of his life, and you don't know what I'm talking about."

"You aren't making any sense."

"Oh? He made it sound so real, too. The different places you'd go to make love, including the waterbed. How much you meant to him until you started to mean too much."

"Is that . . ." She lit another cigarette.

"Is that what, Sharon? Why he broke it off? Why he moved her in?" She said nothing. "Sure it is. You should

70

have known." Still she said nothing, but her face seemed to relax. "Kind of ironic of you to put her in the waterbed."

"What on earth are you talking about?"

"You don't think you're going to get away with this, do you? You still have the key to the apartment—and you can't deny that phony ruse to get all those people on the waterbed."

She stood up. "Do you really think *I* killed her?"

"Yes."

For a moment her face showed panic, as though her foot had slipped while climbing a cliff, but she quickly found her balance. "Please leave."

"Tell me about it. Then I'll leave." She shut her mouth and her eyes. "Give me the keys to Phillip's apartment, then."

"I don't have any keys."

"You're lying, Sharon. Little girls who lie don't go to heaven."

"Get out! Get *out* of my house!" she yelled—and then ran from the room.

I got up to go. The screen door slammed and Petey stood in the foyer with a water pistol in his hand. He backed up warily as I walked toward the door and for a moment I thought he might bite me and give me rabies. I didn't care. "Go ahead, Petey," I told him, crossing the porch. "Shoot."

Hunter didn't even move as I drove past him in my truck and I wondered if our little scheme would work. Sharon was upset enough, I thought. It was possible that even a man with the confidence of a Richard Hunter could follow her without bungling it.

71

8

The exercise with Sharon must have given me an appetite,
because I drove to a new restaurant on Colfax Avenue. It
was part of a chain of restaurants and the map of Colorado
on the glossy menu cover had been appropriately distorted
to include all the important places in the state—namely,
towns fortunate enough to hold a link in the chain. Another byproduct of Urban Renewal, I thought. More lead
in the snow.

I ordered steak and eggs. The meat was cut in a neat little square as though punched out by a machine, and the
eggs looked like white saucers with yellow golf balls set in
the center. Naturally I expected the worst, which is a habit
I have cultivated in order to save myself from disappoint-
ment; but the funny thing was, it tasted good. Afterward,
I drove to the Oilmen Club Building for my appointment
with Robert Dix.

A man I recognized as Dix was shouting when I walked
in, and I had the odd sensation of coming in during the
middle of a play I'd seen before. "Woman, we've been
together twenty-five years," he bellowed at the tiny lady
I'd already met. "Can't you read my writing yet?"

"Don't call me 'woman,' Robert. My name is Stella. I
will not have you take that tone with me."

"My dear creature. At home you may be my wife. Down here you are an employee of Great Mesa Shale, which I happen to own. If I choose to call you 'woman,' then I will by god call you 'woman!'" He flung a paper at her. "Now. Woman. Type that letter again, and this time, do it properly!" He stomped into an office and slammed the door.

The lady fumbled for her purse, pulled out a small handkerchief, and dabbed at her eyes. "Come in, Mr. Tree," she said. "I expect you want to see Robert?"

"I can come back, Mrs. Dix."

"That won't be necessary. I'm fine—and so is he, actually. And he's expecting you." She rose to her feet. "He isn't like that often, Mr. Tree. The events of the last few months have disheartened him terribly." She ushered me into his office.

"Well, Tree, come in. Sit down," Dix said. "I knew your father." The man looked as young as his picture, just as his wife had said the day before. "A fine man, your father, although personally I never liked him. That don't take away from his achievements, of course."

I snorted and sat down in a leather chair in front of the low table Dix sat behind. From his high-backed swivel chair he could reach everything in the small room: the massive rolltop desk behind him on the wall, a floor lamp at one end, and Venetian blinds at the other. He was sixty-one or two, although his body and face and voice bristled with the force and power of a much younger man. But there was a bitterness about him deeper than mine, and I wondered if the old bastard enjoyed humiliating his wife.

"You're defending that young radical, aren't you, Tree? Think you can get him off?"

"That's hard to say."

"You lawyers are a constant source of amazement to me. How can you defend a fellow like that? A Communist— worse yet, an anarchist—or even worse, a mutton-headed Liberal! Imaginative, though. Give him that. Not just any-

73

one will dispose of a body by stuffing it in a waterbed!"

"You've been following the case?"

"You bet your life! That young fellow has succeeded in depriving me of everything I've worked for during the last thirty years. When they hang him, believe me, I'd like to pull the lever." He smiled. "I was acquainted with Cora Shannon, too. Puzzling thing about her."

"What puzzles you?"

"A charming young woman, Tree, and a very competent geologist. What the devil did she see in a yahoo like Garver?"

"You knew they were living together?"

"Of course! It was in last night's paper. Something too about an odor—a recognizable odor—a reporter detected on your breath." He smiled again. "Your father wasn't a lush, was he, Tree?"

"Then you didn't know until last night that the Shannon girl had been living with Garver?"

"Now how in the devil would I know that? I was of the impression the corpse's name was JoAnn White."

"When was the last time you saw her, Mr. Dix?"

"Early fall of last year. She was tramping around my property with all the modern divining rods the youngsters use nowadays—spectographic this, electromagnetic that— hogwash, most of it, where oil shale is concerned. You can *see* it. You don't need to explore for it, like you do with oil."

"Isn't oil shale under the ground?"

"Come along, Tree, and I'll show you what I mean." He climbed easily out of his chair and marched out of his office, past his wife, and into another room. "How are you coming on that letter, woman?" Before she could reply he shut the door. "My wife," he said to me. "A wonderful, understanding woman—if your taste runs to wonderful, understanding women—but she don't type worth a damn. I may have to let her go." Maps and charts were pinned to the walls and he fished around in the drawers of a table,

74

thumbing through large, glossy photographs. "Here." He selected three of them, spread them on a work table and turned on a light. They were of cliff faces, taken from the canyon below. Some stunted pine grew like sagebrush on the canyon floor and here and there on a ledge of the cliff a tree fought for a hold. "See that rock? It ain't really oil shale, by the way. Promoters call it that just to whip up enthusiasm. It's really organic marlstone, and if you look close you can see a belt of it about a hundred feet from the top of those ridges, and it runs all the way around and through them. See it?"

"Yes."

"That's the Mahogany Ledge, Tree. Runs thirty to a hundred feet deep in there. One of the richest beds of oil shale anywhere in the world. Of course, that picture ain't on my property, but mine's just like it. You can *see* it."

"Any photos of yours?"

"They're all in evidence. Exhibits, at that trial, where that judge told me I couldn't go onto my own land and mine the oil shale out." He glared at me as though I'd had something to do with it. "He said something about 'due regard to the environment.' Well look at that land! It ain't fit for anything anyway!" His head wandered back and forth. "Ever hear the expression 'piss ant,' Tree?"

"Yes. I've heard it."

"Know what it means?"

"No sir."

"Well, it's a contraction, just like 'don't' or 'can't,' for 'piss on it.'"

I nodded my understanding, which he seemed to require before proceeding.

"Now. Ever hear of the Piceance Basin?"

"That's where all the oil shale is, isn't it?"

"Correct. Now. Do you know how the Piceance Basin got its name?"

"No sir."

"Well, it's a French word that means 'piss ant.' When

the French trappers were over in that country about 1800, they saw all those miles and miles of god-forsaken land and they said, 'Piss ant.'"

I laughed.

"You've been over there, Tree?"

"Many times."

"Well, what do you think of it? Worth bleeding over?"

I thought of the massive rock-canyon walls cut by the Green River, through the high plateaus on the Western Slope. Eerie country. We called it "the badlands" when I was a boy. But it can cast a spell over you if you let it. I've fished and hunted and camped in there, alone and with Joe Reddman, which is the same as being alone—and it can turn you into an Indian. I wondered if all the oil in the world was worth making it over as an anthill.

"Answer my question, Tree. Is it worth bleeding over?"

"I don't know."

"You don't know. Well, if you ask me, those French trappers were right. Piss on it." I had the impression he meant the whole world.

"Cora Shannon worked for Dolores Petroleum, didn't she, Mr. Dix?" I asked, when we had settled back into chairs in his office.

"That's right."

"Wasn't Dolores Petroleum trying to buy your land?"

"They were trying to steal it, Tree. They still are."

"What do you mean?"

"That fellow Drake is a fraud. Oh, he don't look like one, I'll grant you. He has pearly teeth and smiles more than is necessary, and he has that rare ability of presenting you with his profile. He's one of them Madison Avenue oil men, Tree. The industry's full of them now."

"Why is he a fraud?"

"He's trying to get something for nothing. Now don't that make him a fraud?"

"What's he trying to get?"

76

"My land, which is worth a hundred million dollars if it's worth a cent, and he's trying to buy it for fifty!"

"He told me," I said. "Aren't his values based on Cora Shannon's report?"

"That report's a lie. I don't know who wrote it. I *do* know when she was on my land, she told me how rich it was."

"Have you talked to her about it since the report?"

"No. I talked to *Drake* about it and he always promised to have her there, but for some reason she never was."

"Mr. Dix, are you telling me that Dolores Petroleum surveyed your land for oil shale and then gave you a false report about it?"

"That's exactly what I'm saying. Now don't that make him a fraud?" He jumped out of his chair as though galled by an insult. "Woman!" he bellowed, stomping to the door and opening it. "Come—"

"I can hear you, Robert. What is it?"

"Where's that assay report from Dolores Petroleum?"

"You threw it away, Robert."

"Well, why in the devil did you let me do that?" He slammed the door and marched back to his chair. "Twenty-five years I've been married to that woman. Twenty-five years she's been throwing things away, just because *I* throw them away, even though she knows I'll need them sooner or later. You married, Tree?"

"No."

"Want a wife? You can have mine for next to nothing. Well, it don't matter. I can tell you what's in that report anyway." He lit a cigar. "It describes my land, first of all. Thirty-seven miles from Rifle, four sections, near the headwaters of Piceance Creek. Four sections of land is a little more than twenty-five hundred acres, and the rock in there assays out to seventy gallons to the ton, and that is rich." His eyes fixed on mine, locking them in. "According to Drake, I got only half that. He reports subterranean nacolyte—salt zones—but if they're there, how come they

77

don't show on the ridges?" He glared at me, apparently expecting me to answer his question. "That report shows my land has about four hundred million barrels, running around thirty-five gallons to the ton. Well, if that's all I have, why has he offered me fifty million dollars and hinted he'd go all the way to sixty?"

"You'll have to educate me, Mr. Dix."

"That don't surprise me," he said. "Now. The price of oil is right at ten dollars a barrel and it should stay that way a few years. But oil *in situ*—meaning before it's been mined, where it stands in the ground—sells for only ten or eleven cents a barrel. That's why if you have a billion barrels, which I have, the price should be a hundred million dollars. But if you have four hundred million barrels, which Drake claims is all I have, the price should be forty million dollars. Now Drake has the same thing as offered me sixty. That is fifteen cents a barrel and it don't sell, *in situ*, for that much."

"Has he told you why he's so high?"

Dix snorted. "Says his tests show my shale has a high nitrogen content, so the spent shale could be sold as fertilizer. Hogwash. Says, too, his engineers have designed a solar energy-powered retort! Pure nonsense."

"The retort is the name for the furnace the rock is dumped in, isn't it?"

"Here's what happens, Tree. The rock with kerogen in it —you know what kerogen is?"

"Kind of a gummy oil, isn't it?" I asked.

"You could call it that. Actually it's a wax-like petroleum product similar to oil, and it's found in the so-called oil shale, which ain't really oil shale at all but organic marlstone. Now. A retort is really a great big kettle that the rock is dumped into, and it's heated, and the kerogen is boiled out of it.

"Now. If Drake has an economically feasible solarpowered retort, then about any oil shale land he could get would be valuable. Not just mine. But he tries to tell me he's willing to pay fifteen cents a barrel, because he can afford to on account of that retort!"

"And you don't believe that?"

"I do not. Another thing. If the shale on my land runs to only thirty-five gallons to the ton, then it isn't worth as much as the shale that runs seventy gallons to the ton. You can see that, can't you, Tree?"

"I can see that," I said. "You'd have to process twice as much rock for the same amount of oil."

"That's right. And from an engineering point of view, if what you're mining runs to only thirty-five gallons to the ton, that's close to marginal stuff. If you get much below thirty, it don't pay to mine it because you can't come out ahead. Now if my land assays at thirty-five gallons to the ton, then a lot of it has got to be less than thirty, because I *know* the rock on the ridges is seventy and eighty!" He leaned forward, and the gleam in his eye radiated venom. "That assay he sent me was doctored. There's another one somewhere—a real one—and believe me, I'd like to get my hands on it." I got up to leave. "Something else you should know, Tree. I've checked on Dolores Petroleum. If Drake paid me sixty million dollars, he'd have to borrow ten."

"What do you mean?"

"I mean he's offered me more than he has. Which means he's offered all he can."

"I still don't understand."

"One of the reasons I never liked your father, Tree, was this thickness about him. Now. You're a lawyer. See if you can follow this. If all Dolores Petroleum can come up with is sixty million dollars, then wouldn't it be to their advantage to make sure my property isn't worth any more than they can pay?"

"I can follow that."

"Then can you understand why I think William Drake is a fraud?"

79

9

There was a time when private investigators called themselves private investigators, but television has changed all that. Now they go by such high-flying titles as "confidential consultants," or "human research bureaus," or names that suggest a connection with the FBI. It isn't surprising. Undertakers have done the same thing. So have housewives, lawyers, and termite exterminators.

But Joe Reddman still calls himself a private investigator. He doesn't watch television enough. A few minutes after leaving Robert Dix, I climbed the stairs of an old building on Capitol Hill and knocked on the door to Reddman's office.

"Come in."

He sat behind his desk, leaning forward with his hands out of sight, as though reading a comic book in class. "What's the matter?" he said when he saw who it was. "Can't you even get that PR outfit to take it?"

With clothes on, Joe looked thin, but I've seen him play handball and he's not. His stomach is flat and hard and his shoulders and legs are as sinewy and lithe as those of a circus acrobat. I sat down on the grimy couch beside his desk and watched as he shoved a pistol into his shoulder holster. Joe has always enjoyed playing games. "They took

80

it," I said. "I have a little detail in mind, though. I think it's just right for you."

His face had been altered by the kind of life he led, but it was still smooth except for the scars, and deeply browned. His eyes were the pure blue color of a mountain sky, and were usually just as blank. "I don't trust you, Nathan," he said.

"It's a burglary," I told him. "You'll enjoy it."

"Huh!"

I told him about my interview with Robert Dix, and that William Drake may have falsified an assay of Dix's land. Somewhere there should be the real report, I said, or at least evidence of it. Drake was still trying to buy the land, and if he got it, he'd need to know what he really had. Probably it would be hidden somewhere in his office.

"All right, I'll go see," he said.

"Good." I got up to leave.

"Wait a minute, Nathan. You'll have to go with me."

I cleared my throat. "Burglary isn't my line."

"I'll be damned. I thought you were a lawyer."

"What do you need me for?"

"I don't know what an assay report looks like."

I thought it over, which was a mistake. My first inclination was to say "no." "All right. When?"

"Tomorrow night. Call you about eleven." He rummaged through his desk, pulled out a knife, and started digging out the dirt beneath his fingernails. "Fingernails are a pain in the ass," he said.

Georgia Robinson lived in an integrated neighborhood not far from City Park, in a huge, porticoed granite stone mansion that had been made over into apartments. I walked up the stairs to the third floor and found her unit in the back, facing the mountains. She was expecting me: I'd telephoned first. The door opened before I could knock. "Come in," she said. All she had on was a pair of Levi shorts, torn fashionably just beneath the pockets, and a T-shirt. She wasn't wearing a bra.

It caused me to smile and feel warm. The T-shirt might have fit me, but it was much too small for Georgia. She poured coffee and we sat in two Danish chairs around a low table, where we looked out a large window toward the mountains. A high-pressure bubble had formed over them and a cleansing breeze had swept the town clean, and the vast bulk of Long's Peak dominated the scene from her window. It shimmered in cool splendor, forty miles away. "A nice view," I said.

She nodded, jiggling her breasts, which I tried not to notice. "I just love it," she said. "Long's is such a magnificent mountain, especially in the winter, when it's absolutely white with snow. Yet if you look over the windowsill you can see garbage in the alley." She picked up her coffee cup. "What a marvelous contrast." I looked at her legs and smiled, and let her talk.

Her family lived in a rich suburb near St. Louis, and she'd come to Colorado to go to school. She was now a graduate student at the University of Denver, where she taught a Freshman English course, worked toward a doctorate in English literature, and embroiled herself in various Causes for the Sake of Mankind. Her expression became lofty, but I didn't mind. She was so young.

"Why did you want to see me, Mr. Tree?"

So I spoiled it, naturally, which is a talent of mine. "I understand you and Watt Chambers were roommates."

She set her cup down quietly, as though she'd expected something like that. "Do you have a reason for bringing up that particular part of my past, or are you just out for kicks?"

"His fingerprints were found in Garver's apartment."

She struggled with it. "How do you know?"

"The DA's office."

"I don't believe you," she said, shutting her eyes like the

monkey who refuses to see evil. "Are you implying Watt had something to do with JoAnn's murder?"

"It's an easy mistake to make, Georgia," I said. "He was killed the same night she disappeared too."

"Why would he do such a thing? He didn't even know her."

"Maybe for money," I said. She didn't move. "He had a record. He could have been a contract killer." The lids over her eyes tightened. "It takes a special kind of ruthlessness to kill for money, young lady. You knew him. Did he have it?"

"How should I know?"

"Tell me about him, then."

Her voice had grown flat, like distilled water. "Different. Usually tender and loving and—grateful—but sometimes cruel and vengeful. I think I was someone else to him then, and he was paying me back."

"How long did it go on?"

"Three months. I had an apartment on Clayton Street and he just sort of drifted in and stayed."

"And?"

"One day he drifted out. He said he'd stayed long enough because all he wanted was a taste, not the habit." Tears formed in her eyes, making them large. "I don't know if it was love, or what, but I made a terrible scene. I just couldn't seem to let go." Angrily she brushed at her face. "I followed after him like a lovesick puppy, begging him to come back—and then one night he did. He wasn't alone, though. He brought two of his friends, and the three of them . . . It was pretty awful."

It felt as though my chest had suddenly been pumped empty, and I must have stared at her.

"That shocks you, doesn't it?" she said.

"Damn right."

"It shouldn't. That's the way we've been treating their women for centuries."

"Good for you, Georgia!" I said. "You had it coming

83

because of all those terrible things other people have done, so you took it. What a service." She didn't answer. "The friends—blacks?"

"Yes."

"What were their names?"

"James Leroi and a horrible little man they called 'Little Dave.'" All at once she covered her face. "Please don't tell my parents."

My chest went hollow again. She probably thought she was free of them and all they stood for, but there they were, on top of her mind. "Did you see him after that?"

"No."

"When he lived with you, did he work?"

"No. He painted a lot, but mostly he just—did nothing."

"What about money?"

"He used mine unless he had some of his own, which wasn't often. I don't know where it came from."

"Ever hear any gossip about Phillip and Sharon Garver?"

"What kind of gossip?"

"An affair."

"It's absurd and vicious to suggest anything like that," she said.

"That may be, but is it true?"

"No."

"What can you tell me about Gene Carruthers?"

She shrugged. "He has money. He's a psychological engineer, whatever that is. And he wants desperately to save the world."

"Crazy, in other words?"

"No more than anyone else."

I thought of the bespectacled little man who lived below Garver at the Gates Tower. Another of mankind's many saviors. "This 'psycho-technological application of drugs.' Do you know anything about it?"

"It's a project he's been working on for years."

"What is the project?"

84

She stared at me quizzically. "You don't know?"

"No."

"He's been experimenting with drugs to suppress aggressive behavior, and has been trying to devise some way to put them in Denver's water supply."

"What? Are you serious?"

"That makes him crazy in your eyes, doesn't it, Mr. Tree? To have the desire to . . ." Suddenly her shoulders were shaking and she couldn't seem to stop them.

I wanted to run, but didn't. "Hey," I said, putting a hand on her arm. In a half-hearted way she tried to push it off, but I wouldn't let her. It occurred to me the two of us had a lot in common: her ideals had led her into situations she'd like to forget, which is about all mine had ever done for me; and she had even come to hate herself. "You mind if I sound like a father?"

"My goodness. I believe you are going to give me the benefit of your years and years of experience."

"Something like that. You know what I think?"

"Tell me. What do you think?"

"I think your head is at an angle, Georgia—kind of like mine—but your heart is on straight."

"How nice." Her voice was gentle and sad.

"Some day, when your head lines up right, you know what?"

"No. What."

"You'll have lots of what us old fogeys call 'class.'"

Eugene Carruthers had leased a building a few miles south of town on Santa Fe Drive, and I found it about four that afternoon. The Rampart Range and Devil's Head Mountain loomed blue and calm in the distance, against a backdrop of white clouds that had started to move in; and the scattering of old buildings, abandoned cars, and rusted junk along the road looked like land that had reclaimed itself from some prehistoric Urban Renewal project. It was a pleasant thought.

85

The building—more of a shed with corrugated metal ceiling and walls—held an assortment of machines, benches, and sinks. Lab equipment was scattered everywhere, and along one wall several rabbit hutches stood in tiers. An office of sorts had been carved out of a corner, and when I walked in Carruthers was slouched behind a rickety desk reading a journal. He was the only person there.

"Well! Nice to see you, Mr. Tree," he said, standing and offering his hand. "Sit down. Sit down." He wore a tweed sport jacket with leather patches over the elbows, sucked on a pipe, and peered at the world through thick glasses, as though mildly astonished at the view.

I found a cardtable chair and pulled it near his desk. You don't look like a mad scientist, I thought. You look more like some mother's precious little thirty-year-old boy. "An unusual setup," I said, trying to decide on the best way to open him up.

"Can I show you around?"

"Let's talk first." He blinked uncertainly. "I'm having trouble figuring you out."

"Well. Does one ever truly know one's fellows?"

"Probably not. Still, you seem intelligent and balanced —oriented, you'd call it—yet you work out here in an old shed, on strange projects, like some kind of mad scientist."

"Well. And that seems eccentric to you?"

"You could say that. And this psycho-technological application of drugs to curb aggression does too. I thought you were kidding at Garver's party, but I've heard since you're serious."

"Of course." His eyes flared, as though someone had tossed a pinch of gunpowder into the fire. "The earth *is* dying, you know. And the principal villain is the nature of man. If we can't curb our aggressive, acquisitive attitudes, we shall *bury* ourselves in our own waste."

"Do you believe that nonsense?"

"Well! Do you mean you don't? Look at what's happening, Mr. Tree! Open your eyes! Irreversible levels of toxicity are building—in our mountains, our oceans, our rivers and streams!"

"Don't you think our instinct for survival will bring us through? This modern emphasis on ecology, for ex—"

"Not nearly enough. Not nearly. The truth of the matter is that all the ecologists, the Phil Garvers, are merely staving off the inevitable. Man's very *nature* must be treated before any worthwhile, lasting change in the environment can be effected." He glared at me as though my blindness infuriated him. "The Phil Garvers of this world, with their phobic attention to symptoms, are actually doing us all a grave disservice."

"How?"

"It's so simple. A certain level of ecological catastrophe is what we need, but their misguided efforts may stave off the small ones until it really *is* too late." When he saw my expression, he tried to be patient. "It's the psychology of crisis. The Communist countries were quite masterful in their use of it, until they developed their own establishment and became more interested in stability. Give the people a cause—a war for example, or a scapegoat—and let them unify in their efforts to defeat whatever it is they think is the enemy."

"I still don't understand."

He smiled, knowing it was no use. "It's so simple. If one natural disaster after another occurs, then possibly the masses will become desperate enough to do the one thing that can save them, which is what I happen to advocate." He settled back, having lost interest in his dissertation. "I'm sure you didn't drive all the way out here to debate my thesis, however."

"You're right. I wanted to ask you some questions about the night JoAnn White disappeared."

He smiled. "Needless to say, I remember it quite well."

"It was Monday a week ago, wasn't it?"

"Yes."

87

"What happened?"

"First, I must set the stage. You know, of course, that I live at the Gate? Phil is on the sixth floor and I am on the third?" I nodded. "Well, I should say twenty minutes before ten—just before the commercial—I was watching 'Gunsmoke.' That particular show is something of a vice with me," he said, smiling again. "Phil called—quite a crucial point in the story—and told me he had to drive to Castle Rock and that JoAnn seemed upset about it. He wondered if I'd mind coming up to his apartment and staying with her until he got back.

"Quite frankly, I suspected a little ploy on JoAnn's part. Just a slight suggestion of dependence there, the little girl afraid to be left alone by her he-man. Consequently I was not in a huge hurry to give up my favorite television show and go rushing up to watch Dean Martin. So I told Phil I'd be up as soon as 'Gunsmoke' was over."

"Go on."

"Well. When it was over I didn't even wait for the preview of the next episode, so I must have been knocking at her door one or two minutes before ten." He sucked at his pipe. "I'm certain I heard something—a scuffling noise—so I called her name and banged on the door, but nothing happened. I must confess it angered me greatly to be left standing in the hall. So I left."

"Did you try later?"

"I telephoned and got no answer, of course. But I didn't go back up the stairs."

"Why not?"

"It didn't seem that anything could be gained by it, because, as I said, I thought she was playing games. I didn't want to get drawn into it."

"Did you see Phillip later?"

"About midnight he woke me up. I, of course, told him JoAnn wasn't in my apartment, that I assumed she was in his, and he said, 'If she is, she must be in the waterbed.'"

"Phillip said that?"

"*Yes*. Well, we both agreed nothing serious could have happened—the security in the building is quite good—and then I told him he needn't worry anyway, that probably she was simply trying to show him how much he missed her. She's just baiting a marriage trap, I said."

"Which is what you thought at the time?"

He nodded. "*Since* that time, however, I've been—tortured, really—by other thoughts. That oddly prophetic remark. Further, my inability to say of my own knowledge that Phil even went out that night. *He might have been there the whole time!*"

"You think he killed her?"

"I find that as hard to believe as everything else."

"What can you tell me about JoAnn? Did you know who she really was?"

The pipe came out of his mouth and he looked at it. "Quite a complex person, but then I suppose you could say that about anyone who manages to get themself murdered." I waited. "In specific answer to your question, no, I did not know who she was. But I never quite believed she was who she said she was, either."

"Who did she say she was?"

"JoAnn White, graduate student at the University of California. Born and raised in Bridgertown, Missouri, where her father owned the bank."

"Why didn't you believe it?"

"She also said she was an only child, but she obviously wasn't. 'Big sister,' or 'little mother'—the stamp of the firstborn child of a large family—was written all over her. And she was far too success-motivated to have come from such a secure background."

"Were you in love with her?"

He blushed. "I hardly think that matters."

"Oh? Jealousy is a fairly acceptable motive for murder. If Phillip really did go out Monday night, how do I know you didn't kill her yourself?"

89

His laugh was short and nervous. "You don't believe that," he said.

The reaction struck me at once. I wondered if it was the normal guilty response of your average everyday psychologist or . . . when all at once I realized how much he looked like Timothy. Lord. He was dumpy, four-eyed, and getting bald, and when you scratched off the façade he showed the same bewildered look that had fastened on Tim. "Why shouldn't I believe it?" I said.

"Really. This is ridiculous. How on earth could I have managed it, picking up a dead body and stuffing it inside a waterbed? I'm simply not that strong."

"How did you know she was dead first?"

He licked his lips. "I didn't. I just assumed . . . Are you serious?"

"Do you have a waterbed, Gene?"

"Yes, but it's not at all like Phil's. His is quite a superior model. It's the only kind I know that has a repair kit that actually works."

"I expect Phillip showed you how to operate it?"

"My gosh. I see how these things happen. I really see."

"What are you talking about?"

"Just the way such seemingly innocent circumstances can point the finger of guilt at one." He tried to look at me. "Phillip *did* show me his repair kit," he admitted.

"Let's switch to something else," I said. "How far along are you in your planning?"

"Planning?"

"Peace on Earth. The injection of chemicals into Denver's water supply."

He looked apprehensive, as though taking off for the first time in a space ship. "Did you hear about that?"

"That's rather obvious."

He cleared his throat, then talked in a low voice, as though confessing a crime. "I've encountered technical difficulties. You see, the ratio of water to chemical ingested is crucial, and I am presently unable to devise an accurate way of controlling it."

"You're still working on it?"

"Well . . . Would it do any good to tell you something?"

"I don't know."

"Do you remember the Berrigan brothers and their conspiracy trial?"

"Not very well."

"Some years ago they were accused of conspiring to kidnap Dr. Kissinger as a protest against the Vietnam war." A sad little clown's smile blinked across his face. "I'm like they were, I think. All this apparatus—I'm quite wealthy, you know, and can afford to indulge my fantasies—but I'm really quite harmless. You must believe me. It's a game and I'd never do it."

I felt like getting drunk. The fellow seemed to want to look guilty, like a martyr in some nameless cause. My staring must have made him nervous, because he started in again, in short little bursts: "I think, considering the circumstances, you know, a body in a waterbed—I don't blame you in the least for being suspicious of me. I'd be looking for a ding-ding of some sort too, I suppose, were I you."

"Now you're telling me you're a ding-ding?"

"Well. Aren't all psychologists supposed to be odd?" He forced a laugh. "That does accord with the general view, and I must say there's a kernel of truth in it."

"Meaning?"

"People are drawn to their professions for reasons, aren't they? Just as people who manage to get murdered attract murderers?" He couldn't quite look at me. "I must confess I got into psychology out of a desire to—to understand myself."

"Did it work?" I asked, standing up.

"I don't know, really."

It was getting on toward five in the afternoon and some

days I'll have a little nipper before six. The chances were pretty good that this would be one of those days. "Do me a favor," I said, walking toward the door.

"Of course."

"Don't get caught, especially for something you didn't do." He looked at me like a timid "yes" man who hangs on every word. "You'd be too easy to convict, Carruthers. It's people like you who give 'justice' a bad name."

The nipper will have to wait, I thought as I drove back to town. Hunter made me wait the customary three minutes before ushering me into his inner sanctum, where he showed me the evening paper. "Autopsy Reveals Murder Victim Pregnant," a headline read. "Now they've got a motive," he said.

He began telling me what he'd found, finding it necessary to speak in the brittle, concise language of a police report. Cora Shannon, alias JoAnn White, petroleum geologist employed by Dolores Petroleum, on sabbatical leave from her job at time of death. Born Bridgertown, Missouri, oldest child in family of six, father the manager of a chain grocery store. Left home after high school for San Francisco, worked as a salesperson in various stores, put herself through University of California in three years. Worked for Wyoco Oil six months, located Casper, Wyoming, but couldn't take the town. Came to Colorado because of oil shale boom, received master's degree in petroleum geology Colorado School of Mines while working full time for Dolores Petroleum. Over-all impression: a looker, competent, hungry for success.

William Drake, founder of Dolores Petroleum Company, from Alder City, Pennsylvania. Father an executive in oil business, retired. Drake a university professor with an MS in engineering, BA in business. Taught at University of Wyoming three years, "Economics of Mining," inherited substantial estate from mother, quit and formed own company. Attracted top people, among them Cora

Shannon. No suggestion of anything more than business relationship between them, however. Drake also attracted big money. Because oil shale development essentially a mining problem, right down his alley. Has been shopping for a property, supporting his company by doing consulting work until he gets what he wants. Has been negotiating for the Great Mesa Shale property in the Piceance Basin, which would cost him everything he's got.

Robert Dix, founder and owner of Great Mesa Shale. A character. Born Glenwood Springs, Colorado, graduated from Colorado School of Mines, 1935. Refused commisson during World War II, went to jump school, was decorated for gallantry in Italy. Predicted present energy crisis in 1947, stating that oil shale the solution, acquired twenty-five hundred acres in Piceance Basin for ten dollars an acre. Has been a fairly successful wildcatter, making enough money to finance his real interest, namely, the development of an economic method of getting oil out of oil shale. Has had great difficulty getting mining patents on his land, largely because of government interference, most of which he brought on himself by refusing to comply with regulations he regarded as "asinine." With increase in price of crude, Dix's method has become economically feasible. He commenced mining shale some months ago, was shut down by a court order. Now actively seeking a buyer for his property, still cussing the government. Will probably sell to Dolores Petroleum, even though he thinks their offer too low.

Barney Madden, a liberated broad, who describes herself as "secretary and driving force behind Clear Sky, whereas Phillip Garver is the figurehead" (quote from May 27 issue of Denver *Chronicle*). Came to Colorado from . . .

"What did Sharon do after I left her?"

"Oh." He found another page. "That was twelve fifteen today, Tuesday, July fourteenth. Subject in a housecoat when you left, fully dressed fifteen minutes later. Drove to a pay telephone on corner of Colfax and Gaylord, made a call, no answer. Kept trying. At twelve fifty-five got an answer, hung up right afterward, sore as hell. Went to Evergreen Bar, Colfax and Corona, drank martinis until two twenty. Drove to Brown Palace Hotel around two thirty-five, sat in lobby, then at a few minutes to three, waited by telephone booth near elevators. At two fifty-eight stepped inside booth, pretended to talk on telephone. At three oh two it rang, she released receiver, talked very intently—but I couldn't hear any of it. At three oh six she left, returned home, still under surveillance by other operatives." He put the page down and grinned.

"She was contacted by someone at the Brown Palace. Right?"

"Right, Mr. Tree. You said she'd lead us to the killer and now, just maybe, we've got it solved for you. Just find out who she's talking to."

"Can you?"

"Depends." He got to his feet and paced the floor, I suppose to add portent to his banalities. "We see this kind of thing all the time. Chances are she'll come back to the same booth for another message and if she does, we got her."

"How?"

"A bug. Slip a little bug in there. Easy."

"Wait until I get a court order," I said.

"What?" He stared at me as though I'd admitted to being a Communist. "Come on, Mr. Tree. You think your killer's going to wait while you get a court order?"

"You'll have to keep her alive, Hunter. Easy."

"Yeah. Well, it would be a helluva lot easier if we knew who was after her."

"Let me explain something to you, young man. It won't do any good at all to get the information if we can't tell anyone about it. But if we do it right, we'll have evidence we can use in court."

"Yeah. Or a dead witness."

I wanted to question Garver about that "oddly prophetic remark," and drove to the county jail. The booking sergeant seemed to think it was funny. "He bailed out, Mr. Tree. This afternoon. Naturally now he's back on the street, we're gettin' ready for a crime wave."

It was after eight when I got back to my office and found a note from Garver under the door:

Nathan: My dad got up the ransom—made a deal with Boston Mutual Bonding, only cost him three or four thou—and I was never so glad of anything in all my life.

I've got to be by myself. Don't know where I'm going—on a private backpack, maybe up around Toklat, although that's pretty crowded—but I'll be back for the preliminary. Oh. You have my authority to do anything you think needs to be done, at your sole discretion, on my behalf, during my absence. How's that? Got it from the lawyer who bailed me out.

If you need money, talk to Dad.

Phillip

Lord, I thought, getting out the whisky and pouring some into a glass. Now my client's got to be off by himself like some kind of pilgrim. I kept pouring whisky into the glass, knowing one drink was all I could afford, so I decided to make it a big one.

It felt good in my stomach, radiating through my body like central heating on a cold day, so I poured the rest of the bottle into the glass. It isn't another drink, I told myself. It's part of the first one. There's no point in punishing myself just because my one and only drink is too large for the glass.

I sipped the whisky more slowly, and enjoyed the hot flow of it as it washed from my mouth, through all those tubes and into my stomach. Then I loosened my tie and wandered to the telephone. Maybe I'll give Sharon a call, I decided, before the whisky takes me out.

"Sharon?" I said a moment later.

"Who is this, please."

"Come come, my dear, you know who I am. I'm the fellow who buried JoAnn White in the waterbed." She said nothing. "Thought I'd tell you, honey. You're next."

"Is this Nathan Tree?"

I took a sip of whisky and thought it over. "Actually, you're right and I'm wrong," I said.

"Are you drunk again? Everyone knows you were drunk in court." I took another sip and thought some more. "Why are you calling me, Mr. Tree? What are you trying to do to me?"

"Actually, I'm trying to save your life." There was no response. "It's your life, of course, and you might say I have no right to interfere. But how long do you think your friend is going to wait?" No reply to that one, either. "He's used you, Sharon. But, as they say, you've outlived your usefulness. He'll . . ."

"Oh!" she said, and hung up.

10

When I rolled over, my head gonged against a piece of metal. I sat up, wondering where in hell I was, and succeeded in scraping my face against the long thin needles of a Ponderosa pine.

"You jackass," I said to myself. I remembered calling Sharon, then finishing my one and only drink and going out for another bottle, then nothing. Apparently I had nested overnight in the bed of my pickup and had parked the damn thing under a pine tree. I wondered where. It wasn't at my ranch on Shadow Mountain; there are plenty of spruce up there but it's too high for the Ponderosa. I pushed the branches out of the way and climbed down.

The sudden beauty of the scene literally took my breath away. A brilliant clear blue mountain sky washed into the grassy hillside that sloped gently away, and the tall, proud Ponderosa shimmered against the skyline like green flame. It hurt my eyes. I let them burn a moment, then made my way to the cab of the truck, turned it around, and followed my tracks back out.

My head didn't ache exactly. It floated. The blue mountain air had a liquid quality and I felt like a fish, lazing along the bottom of a lake filled with pure, clean water. My tracks connected with a jeep trail that led to a dirt road I'd been on before. I was in the Pike National Forest, thirty miles southwest of Denver.

The good feeling didn't last. An hour later, when I parked in front of my office, I wanted to die. Once inside I dropped to my hands and did pushups until my body vibrated with effort, then collapsed to the floor. Sweat jumped through my skin and I thought I might get lucky and throw up, but couldn't manage it. I did more pushups, then showered and dressed.

It was ten o'clock when Ada Little bustled me into Rollander's office. The tall trail deputy was having a conference with a coarse-faced detective who remembered me from the old days, but whose name I couldn't recall. We told reciprocal lies about how nice it was to see each other, and he left the room.

Rollander was contented that morning, as though he'd just convicted someone of murder. It made me suspicious. I tried to draw him out, but couldn't get past his grin. I told him I needed a court order for the bugging of a telephone booth at the Brown Palace, but under the statute only a DA could get one. He said he'd have it that afternoon, but made me agree to give him a duplicate copy of any tape.

I dropped by the RMBI office to tell Richard Hunter, but his secretary told me he was out. I waited—it gave me a chance to sit down; half an hour later she woke me up. Hunter's feet were on his desk when I walked into his office and he didn't bother about getting up. Apparently our relationship had entered a new phase. "Get a good sleep?" he asked as I sat down.

"Good enough."

"Well, sleep them off somewhere else."

I was surprised by his remark. Maybe it was because of the floating I'd done earlier, but just then he seemed very young. I could remember how it felt. "Sorry."

"Forget it."

"Feel like talking things over?"

"Hey. Good idea, Mr. Tree. A lot of angles to this case, maybe some you haven't thought about." He put his feet down and concentrated on my face. "I think we can blow it wide open for you."

"Oh?"

"Yeah. Take Sharon Garver and her mysterious telephone calls, for example. Or Watt Chambers and those fingerprints of his in the closet. Or JoAnn White, alias Cora Shannon, the tool—maybe the victim—of Big Oil. See what I mean?" He grinned with the supreme confidence of a promoter. "We parade red herrings in front of that jury, boggle their minds, you line up character witnesses, let me do the rest. We can walk that guy out of there easy."

"Another way is to find out who killed the girl."

He laughed. "We already know," he said. "Our job is to get him off."

An ant appeared on the edge of Hunter's desk and made its way toward the center. I wondered how an ant had gotten into such a tidy office. "You weren't so sure about it yesterday, Richard. What changed your mind?"

"Common sense. Plus talking to the boys in homicide. They got it locked pretty tight."

"Let's hear it."

"They figure it happened Monday night, July sixth. They have witnesses can prove she was alive that day, wasn't seen again until Saturday night, July eleventh, when her body got fished out of Garver's waterbed."

"Go on."

"They can put Cora and Garver in his apartment that night, too. They can also prove neither of them went out."

"How do they do that?"

"Nobody saw them leave."

"You've been there, haven't you? How much traffic in the building, especially around ten o'clock on a week night?"

"Okay, Mr. Tree. Not conclusive. Still, nobody saw Garver leave or come back—and nobody saw anybody come *in* the building that night, either. No strangers or weirdos, I mean."

"If you had keys, how hard would it be for you to get in Garver's apartment without being seen?"

"Not very hard, I admit. Check the lobby before going in. Take the stairs instead of the elevator. Still, some luck involved. Out of all the chances, you'd think someone in that building would have seen something."

"Anything else?"

"They figure it took at least an hour to kill her, drain enough water out of the bed for the body, put her in, and seal it up. Who else had the time?"

"Very astute."

"They also got motive. Garver knocked her up, found out about it, killed her. Or he found out she was an oil company spy, so he killed her. Or both. Then he hid her body in the waterbed, probably planning to move it when he had the time."

The ant stopped at a piece of paper, examined it with its antennae, and started across. I wondered if walking on paper felt different to the ant from walking on wood. "They keep asking themselves, why would anyone put her in the waterbed? Why not just kill her, leave her on the floor? Anybody except Garver, that is." Hunter's eyes picked up the ant and for a moment the little creature seemed to sense danger and scurried and zigged. Then Hunter's thumb lit on its back.

"The way the body was found?" I asked. "All those barefoot people, standing around on the waterbed?"

"Parties like that, anything can happen." He scraped the remains of the ant off his thumb and into a wastebasket. "Maybe Garver's a little dippy too. You know, the perfect crime syndrome. Bravado, plus an unconscious need to get caught."

"What about Chambers's fingerprints?"

"The police can put him in Garver's apartment five months ago."

"Would prints last that long?"

"No reason why not. The closet wasn't used that much." He pulled out his pipe, stuck it in a tobacco pouch, and began pressing the fibers into the bowl. "What's your theory, Mr. Tree? Some unknown, mysterious party hired Chambers to kill the girl, put her in the waterbed? Then the mystery man killed Chambers?"

"Something like that."

"No offense, Mr. Tree, but it makes a better red herring." He lit his pipe. "You really think Garver is innocent?"

"I don't know how 'innocent' he is. I just don't think he killed the girl."

"So let's go the red herring route anyway. We win the case, justice is done. Right?"

"No it isn't," I said. "We find out who."

"Come on, Mr. Tree," he said, perhaps louder than he'd intended. I looked at him and his eyes fell away. "Okay, Mr. Tree," he said. "You're the boss."

I got up, wishing he had a window to look out of. "We are going to assume Garver is telling the truth," I said. "The Monday night she disappeared, he told me he drove to Castle Rock on a wild goose chase." I went on, and told him about the telephone call and Garver's wasted trip.

He snorted. "You believe that?"

"Yes."

"The old urgent-message gimmick. How many times have you heard it before, Mr. Tree?"

"Once or twice," I said, remembering the way Garver's tale would have sounded ten years ago.

"Do we know anything about the guy who called?"

"He disguised his voice, so it's probably someone Garver knows."

"No offense, Mr. Tree, but the mysterious caller bit, they always disguise their voice." He doodled on a sheet of paper and I wished my head would clear up so I could

101

think. "What do you want to do?" he asked. "Work up a profile of our killer, based on what we think we know?"

"Sounds good."

"Okay. He's an amateur, which is why he had to hire Chambers." He made a note. "Come to think of it, why am I saying 'he'? Could Garver tell if the caller was a man?"

"No."

"So it's a male or female amateur who knows Garver. The creep also knew Garver had a waterbed, knew how to patch it, and probably even knew where Garver kept his repair kit." He took the pipe out of his mouth and kept on writing. "Unless Chambers knew all that stuff." Something in his manner said this was too easy for a man of his talents, like Michelangelo painting a picket fence.

"Not very likely," I said. "He and Garver barely knew each other."

"Well, that's our profile then." He put the pipe back in his mouth and looked at the pad. "Not much, but I guess it's something."

"I want you to find out who hired Watt Chambers," I said, and gave him the names of the two men who had entertained themselves with Georgia Robinson.

"Friends of Chambers?" Hunter asked.

"They shared a common experience. We can also work from the other end."

"You mean possible suspects, right? Only if you don't mind, Mr. Tree, I'll think of them as red herrings."

"Suit yourself."

"So all those people you wanted backgrounds on are red herrings." He opened a drawer, pulled out a file, and found a sheet of paper neatly clipped in. "This could be fun. Take Pete and Sharon Garver. We got the Garver millions to work with there, know what I mean? Pete and Sharon work out an angle to discredit Phil, the fair-haired . . ."

"You're getting tiresome, Hunter." He sucked in his breath and tried to keep anger and contempt off his face.

I'm getting old, I thought, and tried to make it easy by changing the subject. "The DA's office is getting a court order for the bug. They'll have it this afternoon."

"You're talking about the phone booth at the Brown Palace? Sharon Garver?"

"That's what I'm talking about."

"Who puts the bug in?"

"You do. We furnish the DA with a duplicate tape."

"Thought there'd be a catch," he said, holding his pencil over his desk and dropping it. "What if it turns out to be Sharon's lover, some little dealy-bob like that? No connection?"

"Then we'll know there's no connection."

"Yeah. So will the DA. He'd also know all that mysterious behavior of hers doesn't have anything to do with anything, and there goes one of our best—suspects."

"That's right."

He took a deep breath, as though preparing himself to jump into icy water. "You still want to talk?"

"Go ahead."

"I know you have ethical problems, Mr. Tree, and can't put on evidence you know is irrelevant just to confuse things. But what you don't know won't hurt you. So why not let me listen in first? If there's no connection, I just don't pass it on, you can still parade Sharon before the jury as a suspect. If there *is* a connection, we can still get the order and use what I already have."

"Wait for the order."

"Listen. You have a trial on your hands. How come you aren't getting ready for the *trial?* Sure, you believe Garver. But why don't you accept the facts the way they are, then do what you're getting paid to do and acquit the slob?"

The trouble with hangovers is they take the edge off. Instead of firing him on the spot, I started for the door.

"Hope you aren't sore, Mr. Tree."

"Don't worry about it."

"Well, look. You know we aren't gonna corroborate that

weird tale of Garver's, a mysterious telephone call, a trip to Castle Rock. Who's gonna believe that crap? We aren't gonna get around the fact that no one but Garver had a reason to put her body in the waterbed, either. All we have are red herrings: Sharon's mysterious behavior, the Garver family and their millions, maybe something with that Barney Madden broad, maybe something with big oil money. Things like that. See what I mean?"

"No."

"God Almighty, I wish you'd at least *listen*, Mr. Tree." When he saw my face, he backed off into a smile. "Let me tell you how the best criminal lawyers in the East would handle it, okay? *Realistically*." He nodded his head and smiled some more in an effort to get me smiling too. "Okay? Now, who killed the girl, who had a reason, the time, the knowhow? Garver. Fine. Give up on the case? Hell no. That's when you start turning everything into a *mystery*." He stared at me with all the sincerity of a used car salesman, making a rock-bottom offer. "All we have to do is raise a reasonable doubt, Mr. Tree. Why take a chance on the truth?"

I laughed, even though it hurt my head, and walked out.

1499 Pike Street was an old stone mansion, hiding behind a lilac hedge like a buffalo frightened by traffic. I walked a broken flagstone walk to the main door. Some paint had scaled off the poor old wreck, showing like lightning cuts on pine; and the ears and noses on much of the statuary on the rampart on top had been knocked off.

You can know a building by its tenants, and after reading the outdoor directory I thought I knew why this one wanted to hide. What had been a fine old home now housed a free university, an artists' cooperative exhibit, a divine guidance center for the disciples of Marahaj Gishi, and Clear Sky. It made me think of a poster I had seen tacked to a tree in the Eagle's Nest Wilderness Area. "Socialists, Unite!" the thing had proclaimed.

Clear Sky had "Suite F," which was on the second floor, down a dingy hall. I knocked on the door. "Yes," someone on the other side said.

"Barney Madden?"

"Speaking."

"I'm Nathan Tree, Ms. Madden. Can I come in?"

"Certainly."

I'd expected a youthful Amazon, but the woman before me was forty-five, short, and thin. She wore black ankle-length trousers that hadn't been pressed, moccasins, and a sweat shirt. Her face and arms had the leather look of a cowboy and her hair, short and combed straight back, could have been formed out of wire. "There's coffee in the back," she said. "Help yourself."

The small rooms were orderly enough, but dirty. Three desks, four or five file cabinets, and several shelves filled with books were crammed into the main room; and the closet-size room in back held a cot, a sink, an icebox, and another door. It opened into a toilet. A coffee pot and paper cups sat on a small table in the corner. I poured a cup—it looked like oil—and walked back.

The woman had pulled a folding chair out of the space between two file cabinets and opened it for me. "Sit down if you want," she said, seating herself on the edge of one of the desks and lighting a cigarette. "I've heard of you, of course. Quite honestly, I'd have preferred it if Phillip had retained someone else."

I snorted. "Sorry."

"You needn't be. I have the habit of saying what I think —which can be troublesome, but usually saves a lot of time."

Neither one of us tried particularly to charm the other, and we covered a lot of ground in a hurry. She'd never trusted JoAnn White, she told me—not because of her expertise in petroleum geology or her opportune appearance at Clear Sky, but because of the suddenness and depth of her involvement with Phillip. The young woman had admirable self-assurance; she'd not been warped by our peculiar society into a dewey-eyed sex object. Why was she so eager to peel off her clothes and crawl in Phillip's bed?

"Maybe they were in love," I said.

"Ridiculous."

Something about the way she said it was wrong. "Were you jealous?"

"Jealous?" she asked, hopping down from the desk and spreading her arms. "Look at me." She did a small curtsy. "I've about as much sex appeal as Phyllis Diller, but the difference is, I don't *care*."

"You care about something."

"What do you mean?"

"Something about them living together bothered you. The way things are now, why should it?"

"Hm," she said, leaning against the desk. I had the impression she was honestly trying to understand how she felt. "You know, you're right." Thoughtfully, she lit another cigarette. "It must be more than residual prejudice against 'that kind of girl,'" she said. "At least, I hope so. Phillip is a public person—a symbol of so much that's right and good—and perhaps I wanted to keep his image from being tarnished by his nature."

"Maybe you just wanted to mother him."

"You bastard."

"Would you have gone so far as to remove this potential blemish to his image?"

"Absurd."

Suddenly I recognized this woman. The accent was wrong and she smoked a cigarette instead of a pipe, but I still knew her. She was my grandmother, as gutty and single-minded as a billy goat, who came to Colorado in a covered wagon. I'd always kind of liked the old bitch, and she kept Grampa alive a long time after he was supposed to have died, although he may not have thought it was worth it. "Did Phillip have other lady friends, Barney?"

106

"You're talking about that very good variety of friend, I take it?"

"Yes."

"I don't know. I honestly have never considered it my business who he sleeps with and haven't paid any attention."

"What about Sharon Garver?"

"That's a terrible thing to suggest."

"Is it true?"

"Definitely not."

"Were you surprised at who the Shannon girl really was?"

"Very." She dropped her cigarette on the floor and ground it out. "Am I a suspect?"

"I suppose."

"Then let me defend myself, Nathan. I have a theory."

It occurred to me we were calling each other by first names. "Go ahead. Just don't let it get too complicated."

"Have you wondered why anyone—other than a complete madman—would stuff that poor creature into a waterbed?"

"I have."

"It's *just* the kind of thing those ruthless bastards would do. Not to get rid of the girl. They could care less about her. But to destroy Phillip!"

"What ruthless bastards are we talking about?"

"The oil companies. The large ones, with their web of interlocking boards of directors. They're after the world, you know."

"How would putting her in a waterbed help them?"

"There wouldn't be enough *publicity* in simply framing him with some common, everyday kind of murder. But for the corpse of a beautiful girl—especially one connected with an oil company—to be found inside Phillip Garver's waterbed! *That* is the kind of frameup they would do!"

"Garver is that important to them?"

"Of course. We've hurt them in the past, and this Great

107

Mesa victory must have hurt them badly. *They* are bound by the Judge's decision too." Her hands moved beautifully as she talked. They were small, balanced, and stained with nicotine. "Don't you see? To them, *everything is public relations*. How did they get their depletion allowance, for example? By persuading a dull-witted mob of congressmen that public sentiment demanded they get one. Public relations, thought control, power. *That's* the way to rule the world now. And look at the price of oil! The public has been duped into believing those ridiculous amounts of money for gasoline are necessary because of the cost of producing it!" She lit another cigarette. "It's about as difficult to make as distilled water," she said, inhaling deeply. "Their profits are enormous, Nathan. Anyone who threatens those profits is fair game. To them, a business decision, pure and simple. The domino theory in another context: destroy the man who typifies the movement in order to destroy the movement. *That's* why she was put inside a waterbed!"

"Feel better?" I asked.

She glared at me, then smiled. "Yes. I have another theory, too."

"Who's the enemy this time? Alabama?"

"No. Robert Dix."

"Go on."

She leaned forward. "Have you asked yourself why JoAnn—Cora Shannon—was helping Clear Sky?"

"I've wondered about it."

"You'll find that the oil company she worked for was and still is trying to buy that Great Mesa land. Has it occurred to you that the *real* reason JoAnn was helping us was in the hope that if Dix lost, he'd sell his land to Dolores Petroleum? It's for sale now, you know."

"I've heard that."

"Perhaps you don't know how much Robert Dix hates Phillip. Now, suppose Dix had found out what the Shannon girl was really doing. By murdering her and framing it on Phillip, he gets his revenge against the girl and at the same time destroys the man he hates!"

"The other one is better, Barney," I said.

"Oh?"

"It looks like the girl was killed two days before the trial, right?" She nodded. "Then her body was stashed away in the waterbed where it might still be, if it hadn't been for a lucky bet." She looked at me as though I were cheating. "Dix has been in the oil business long enough to know something about public relations too. If he'd killed her, wouldn't it have made better sense for him to make sure her body was found before the trial, instead of three or four days later?"

"Chauvinist."

I smiled, and we sat quietly for a moment. She didn't suffer from the general female compulsion to fill all lapses with sound, and it took a while for me to find out much about her. As a matter of fact, I finally had to ask.

She'd been married to a dentist who developed a comfortable practice in a nice, quiet suburb of Cleveland. Then some years ago she surprised herself, her two teen-aged children, and "the Doctor" by walking out. She hadn't played a game of bridge since, she said, and hadn't missed it. In fact there were very few aspects of her old life she missed, even though she was grateful for having had the opportunity to live it. It gave her a measure of perspective, she thought: a background against which she could contrast and compare the new and old and "different" value structures she encountered as she walked on by, stopping occasionally for a sample like a guest at a wine-tasting party.

You make it sound pleasant and nice I thought, like yachting down the California coast. But I thought, too, that the penetrating flame in her eye told another story. You don't break away from the past without pain, and I wondered if there were any scars.

Then she told me the police had searched the Clear Sky

109

office, and I asked if they'd taken anything. She said they had: one of the three typewriters in the office, and some paper. She didn't know why.

I got up to go. Just for the hell of it, I told her my sympathies were with the oil companies, and that I believed the primary achievement of groups like Clear Sky was to compound the energy crisis. "Nathan, Nathan, Nathan," she said, and I felt like a fly in a web. "Do you know who you remind me of? Really, I wish you could have met him. Super-square, I used to call him, even though he was one of the few men who could make me laugh."

I allowed myself to be drawn into her game. "Who?"

"My grandfather," she said. "Honestly. You even *look* like him."

11

Rollander had promised to have the court order that afternoon, and I parked beside the old West Side court house just before four.

When I saw him in his office, his eyes were cold and hard and no matter how pointedly I stared at his mustache, I couldn't get it to twitch. I asked him for the order and he told me to go to hell. Then he accused me of trying the case in the media, and promised to even the score. I asked him what the problem was but he let me out the door, making it clear he wanted me as bad as he wanted my client.

In a way, it made me feel good. When I was his age I'd been like that, and was glad to know the youngsters could still hate. By some kind of magic my trials were transformed into duels between the other lawyers and me, and now they remembered me as vindictive. I picked up a paper on the corner and looked for whatever it was that had lifted the young cub's back. It was on the front page. "Waterbed Murder Linked to Death of Black Extremist," a headline read, and the story quoted "authoritative sources" to the effect that Watt Chambers might have murdered the woman geologist. Chambers was known to have been in Garver's apartment, according to the report

111

and, furthermore, the black man was believed to have been a hired killer. But no one knew who had hired him, or why.

There was no point in telling Rollander I'd had nothing to do with it, because he wouldn't have believed me. But I had an idea who the "authoritative source" was; and when Hunter's secretary told me she didn't know where he was, I told her she'd damn well better find out. She started to cry. On a hunch I asked her if Hunter had finished that bugging job at the Brown Palace, and her head had started to wag when Hunter broke out of his office and strode into the waiting room.

"Mr. Tree! Saw your truck just now as I came in the back door. Been at the police building." He was all charm. "Man, a lot happening. Come on in." He held his office door for me. "Julie, go on home, kid," he said, shutting the door.

As we sat down a muffled sound came from the intercom system on Hunter's desk. Then we heard the sound of a desk drawer slamming shut. "That old shit! Who does he . . ."

Hunter reached over and clicked it off, then grinned at me. "Must have left my machine on when I went out," he said. "What was that all about? You make a pass at her?"

"You've been in here listening, haven't you? When I asked her about the bugging job at the Brown Palace, you tried to break it up?"

"Honest, Mr. Tree. I just came in."

I nodded slowly, as though I wasn't sure. "Have you seen this afternoon's paper?"

"No sir."

"Could be a break for us," I told him. "A story linking Chambers to the waterbed killing."

"Hey. Sounds all right. Think it'll help?"

"Send a bill, Hunter," I said, standing up. "You're fired."

"Wait!" He jumped to his feet and stared at me like a

112

beggar. "I'm—I'm sorry about that story, Mr. Tree. I just tried too hard."

The last thing I'd expected was an apology.

"Look. Where I worked before, a big case, it was just routine to leak that kind of thing. I did it without thinking. When I told Charlie Riggs, he said you'd blow your stack." He swallowed at something in his throat. "I'm really sorry, Mr. Tree, but man, don't fire me. I want to make it around here."

Watching him suffer wasn't as pleasant as I'd pictured it. "Damn you, Hunter," I said. "Rollander's sore as hell about that story. Now I'll have to fight him for that order."

He took a deep breath and then shrugged his shoulders, as though to say he guessed he'd be moving soon. "Something else I have to tell you, Mr. Tree."

"Go ahead."

"You won't need that order now."

"Why not?"

"This afternoon I hid a little recorder in that phone booth, just to pick up Sharon's end of the conversation. Not a bug or a telephone tap, you understand. I thought maybe that way it wasn't illegal."

"It is. What happened?"

He sat down. "She came in the same time she was there yesterday, had her little conversation, left. One of my agents followed her out, another one got the recorder. He took it to his car, which was parked in an outdoor lot on Lincoln Street, locked it in the trunk. He had to deliver returns on a couple of subpoenas to a lawyer in the Metropolitan Building and when he came back the recorder was gone."

"What? What do you mean it was gone?"

He swallowed again. "The car doors weren't locked. Somebody snuck in the car, jerked out the back seat, got in the trunk, and stole it."

I could feel the hair on the back of my neck and Hunter

looked sick. "How did this somebody know about the cassette?"

"We figure he telephoned Sharon from that balcony above the lobby so he could watch her, see if she was alone. When he saw my man take the cassette out of the booth, he followed him, saw where he put it, took it." Hunter's face was pale but the muscles in his head continued to work. "We blew it, Mr. Tree. All I can say."

I am a sinner, I thought. And one of the troubles with being a sinner is that you are too prone to forgive. It occurred to me Christ must have done something awful. "All right, Hunter," I said, sitting down suddenly and wishing I weren't such a soft-headed jackass. "Now you've screwed everything up, let's try to figure out what further damage you can do."

"I'm not fired?"

"Not yet, anyway. Did you get a description of whoever took the recorder?"

"Yes." A measure of buoyancy seemed to fill his chest and, oddly enough, it made me feel good. "Thanks, Mr. Tree. You're okay."

"What have you got?"

"A bellboy. Been at the Brown thirty years, one of those observers-of-the-human-scene types. Know what I mean?"

"I think so."

"Four days in a row now, always around three in the afternoon, he's seen the same broad hang around the same telephone booth in the lobby. Sharon Garver. So he was watching for her today. Saw my man go in the booth just before Sharon arrived. Then watched Sharon go in a few minutes later, get her call, leave. Saw another one of my men follow her out, then watched as the other one got the recorder.

"Then he says this big guy kind of half trotted down the steps from the balcony—awkward, but moving fast. Heads for the exit my man with the cassette went out of."

"What did he look like?"

114

"Dark glasses, a brown coat that looked too big, boots, a wide-brimmed hat that hung over his face. Out of place looking, the bellboy said, like a mountain man at an opera."

I couldn't seem to get enough air. "Would he recognize him if he saw him again?"

"Doesn't think so, Mr. Tree. Says you could put the same clothes on about anyone and he couldn't tell the difference."

"Did you show him any pictures? William Drake, or Carruthers, or . . ."

"I showed him one, Mr. Tree."

"Who?"

"I got to thinking, with Garver out on bail . . ."

"You showed him Phillip's picture? What did he say?"

Hunter shrugged. "He said, 'Could be.'"

The telephone rang at eleven that night. "You ready?" Joe Reddman asked.

"I've been thinking, Joe. Maybe . . ."

"Damn it, Nathan, you think too much with your head. Doesn't that get tiresome?" I didn't ask him what he meant. Joe's perspective isn't normal, and I didn't want to get into it. "Is it on or off?" he asked.

"On."

"Okay. Put on dark pants, a dark shirt, a hat, and rubber-soled shoes."

"Rubber-soled shoes?"

"In case you have to think with your feet." I cleared my throat. "Don't put anything in your pockets, either. No billfolds, Kleenex, or guns. See you at the corner of Sixteenth and Arapahoe as soon as you can get there. Don't drive, by the way. Any questions?"

"No."

"Eee hah," he said, and hung up.

I put on an old pair of cotton trousers and a work shirt frayed at the cuffs, and found a pair of low-top climbing

115

shoes in the back of the closet. It's insane, I thought, to put my life in the hands of that savage. I found an old hat under the bed, and had a drink. It was substantial. Twenty minutes later, I was there.

An old-fashioned street lamp lit the corner, just as it might have in the 1890's. This one couldn't have been more than a year old, however. It bathed a wide area with soft yellow light, and the scene it illuminated had all the manufactured reality of a Hollywood set. A grassy plaza with stone benches surrounding a brick pool rested serenely in front of the Oilmen Club Building, and across the street an old brick mercantile building with high arches over the windows and elaborate cornices lining the roof stood as a defiant reminder of the past. It had been saved by the Historic Denver Society and housed a chic dress shop, an avant garde movie theatre, the "Swingin' Singles Club," and a New York delicatessen.

Walking through the cool night had felt good, and the whisky made my fingers feel warm. If Joe can do it I can too, I thought. I found him sitting on a bench near the pool, throwing pebbles at the huge, fat trout that lazed like sated pussycats on the bottom. "Look at those fucking subsidized fish," he said. "They don't even move."

I followed him to an alley and without even looking to see if anyone was watching, he marched on down. "Don't look so guilty, Nathan. Somebody'll try to pick you up."

"What?"

"They'll think you're a fag."

Getting in the building seemed too easy. Joe explained that if the doors had been bolted from the inside, you'd need a battering ram to get in. But because of fire regulations, it was against the law to bolt them shut that way. "A good law, too," he said, fashioning a hook out of wire and opening the heavy steel door. "You never know when there'll be a fire."

Joe walked easily up the stairs near the elevator to the main floor, and I snuck along behind. He looked relaxed,

116

as though on his way to an old fishing hole, and I wondered if he ever realized he was a burglar. "Wait here," he said.

"Where the hell are you going?" I whispered.

"Jesus, Nathan. If you get nervous, call a cop." He disappeared into the lobby and three minutes later he was back. "Come on." I followed him into the well-lit space with high ceilings and burnished marble walls. The security guard's sign-out station blocked the hall to the elevators, but no one was there. "We'll ride," he said.

"Won't he see?"

"We have to take the elevator. The stairway doors open only into the stairway, except for the main floor and basement. Once you're in the stairway, you're trapped."

"Damn it, won't he see?"

"Hell yes he will, Nathan. You think they'd hire a blind man?" I started to ask the questions that flashed through my mind, but Joe had started to whistle. "Have a little faith, Nathan," he said.

We got off on the nineteenth floor. It took him less than a minute to open the door to Dolores Petroleum, and we went inside. "We'll start with Drake's office," he said, and glided down the hall as though he'd been there before. "It's the big one, isn't it?"

"Yes."

Joe quickly looked through the room. No safes or file cabinets. "Try the desk," he said.

I did. "It's locked."

He worked quickly now, and when he had it open, he checked the pedestals and drawers for any other locks. He found a false bottom in the main left-hand pedestal drawer. "Hold the flashlight." His fingers explored the edges. "Here it is." I beamed the light on a small keyhole and watched him stick a wire in it as though threading a needle. A moment later it was open.

The report was in a manila envelope on the bottom. It was in the form of a memorandum from Cora Shannon to

William Drake—single-spaced and five pages long, containing an appendix that held surface and sub-surface contour maps, drill log information, and spectographic charts. "This is it," I said, folding it and putting it inside my shirt.

Joe had his finger to his lips. He motioned me to the door to Drake's office, where I flattened myself against the wall. Quickly and silently he put the desk back together, dropped paper into the metal wastebasket, and lit it.

"Gaw-dam! A fire!" someone in the reception area yelped as Joe melted into the flickering shadows. "Shit!" A uniformed guard rushed past us, focusing on the flames, and we slid out the door. "Where's the gaw-dam phone!"

The elevator the guard had used was there. We rode it to the sixth floor, where Joe punched all the buttons and we got off. "All right," he said. "Start thinking with your feet."

I laughed until the tears rolled out of my eyes as we barnstormed down the stairway into the basement, then down the alley and on to Joe's battered jeep six blocks away. Joe smiled, like an Indian at Custer's massacre, and dropped me by my office, still smiling as he drove away. I tried the door to the building but it was locked. I'd followed Joe's instructions to the letter and didn't have the key. My truck was on the street—also locked—so I put the memorandum under a box in the bed of the truck and started searching for something to open the building with. That goddam Indian, I thought, still laughing. I found some wire in the alley and was fumbling with the door when a policeman with his gun drawn came around the corner.

He might have believed who I was, except I started to laugh again. He handcuffed me and took me to jail.

118

12

I didn't feel like laughing the next morning, after spending the night in the drunk tank, on the floor. Reddman must have known I wouldn't have a key too, which was why he'd been smiling when he left me. I was recognized by the detective who questioned me and when I explained to him that it isn't burglary to break into your own damned office, he released me. The building manager had to open my door and I had a drink, then studied Cora Shannon's memorandum.

Much of it was technical, but the conclusions were not. Dix was right. There were a billion barrels of oil on his land, not four hundred million; and the shale was rich—between sixty and seventy-five gallons of oil to the ton—instead of a marginal amount. It meant Drake, for sixty million dollars, was trying to buy a property his own geologist had appraised at a hundred million. I made copies of the report and called Hunter. "Can you meet me at my office this afternoon?"

"Sure can, Mr. Tree. What for?"

"Just be here at two and I'll tell you then. Bring a gun."

At first Drake's secretary told me he was out, but she found him soon enough when I told her it involved some papers her boss had misplaced. He agreed to meet me at two-thirty, at Coffee's Place on Seventeenth Street.

Coffee's Place was a better than average saloon. My dad used to eat and drink there back when Denver was a town, and I've always found it an easy place to relax. The tables were made out of wood and so were the high-backed chairs; the booze has always been good and there have never been any stools at the bar.

Hunter had gone on ahead and was standing at the bar when I walked in. Drake was in a booth; when he saw me he stood up and waved, then shook my hand with both of his and insisted on buying me a drink. I let him. His teeth gleamed white in his bronzed, handsome face and he talked with charm and enthusiasm about nothing, naturally. I laid a copy of the memorandum on the table.

He took a deep breath, then seemed to relax. "Now what?"

"Suppose you start by telling me the truth."

He tried to smile. "How the hell did I get into this?"

"I don't know," I said. "But you're in it."

"I guess you know I lied the other day?"

"The possibility occurred to me."

He stared at the table. "I met Garver a month or so ago, like he told you. Cora brought him to my office and we talked probably an hour. I liked the guy."

"What did you talk about?"

"Mostly about how Cora could help Clear Sky win that lawsuit. We want it as bad as you do, I told him. We're trying to buy the land."

"The memoranda from the Shannon girl—did she write both of them?"

"Yes."

"But the one you sent on to Dix was a fraud, because the land was worth more?"

"Yes." He sighed, like a good sport who's just learned he has cancer. "She didn't want to do it because she'd gotten

120

to like the old bastard. But I convinced her it couldn't really matter to him—he'd get fifty-five to sixty million, which was more than he'd ever need—and the difference between that and what it was worth would make her and me rich. But not if we can't buy it, I told her—and all I could get was sixty million." He drained his glass. "She finally agreed to redo it."

"Then what?"

"That bull-headed old bastard kept insisting the report was wrong. He said it didn't matter; he wasn't going to sell anyway; but it got to him. He'd been nursing that land of his along for more than twenty years, and I guess it hurt him to find out it wasn't worth what he thought." Drake smiled, as though confession was good for the soul. "Maybe that's why he was so reckless in his mining operation. Lost his heart. His dream wasn't what it was cracked up to be, so he went about committing something like suicide."

"Dix told me he tried to talk to the Shannon girl about the report but couldn't. Is that true?"

Drake nodded. "She didn't want to face him about it, so I always made up some excuse."

"You killed her, I take it, so you wouldn't have to split with her?"

He obviously expected the question. "Christ no. I can't even shoot deer." Hunter had moved down the bar and was standing just a few feet away. "Is that report for sale?" Drake asked me.

"No."

"I'm not talking about peanuts, Mr. Tree," he said. "What about a million dollars?"

My reply wasn't as quick as it might have been, which surprised me. "No."

"Guess I'll have to think of something else."

"Is that a threat?"

"I don't know. What can I do?"

121

"You might suddenly find the real report. You can send it on to Dix."

"You'd let me do that? Why?"

"Because I have a heart of gold," I told him. "It would also give you a chance to kill me."

"What?"

"If you were to try something subtle like that, I'd be inclined to think you killed Cora. That could help my case."

"What do you want me to do?"

"Send him that copy." I got up. "Thanks for the drink."

"The paper says Garver's out of jail."

"That's right."

"Sort of funny, Mr. Tree. You think I killed her and I know better. When you find out Garver killed her after all, where will you be?"

"Disappointed, I suppose, but I'll get over it."

I picked up the evening paper, went back to my office, and poured myself a drink. It was as hot as blazes, so I stripped to my shorts and cooled my feet on the rug. There was nothing in the paper about the case, which bothered me, because Rollander had promised to even the score and I'd be disappointed in him if he made idle threats.

The whisky tasted good but I didn't gulp it, and later I called Hunter to see if he'd learned any more about the man who'd spoiled his "operation" at the Brown Palace. He had not. I asked him about Sharon and he said she was still under surveillance, even though she appeared to know now she was being followed. She'd waved at his men that morning as she left to go shopping, and at the Denver Dry Goods had asked one of them to carry her packages. It was apparent to him a contact had been made, he said. And whatever other effect it had on her, it made her feel pretty good.

I poured another drink and called Joe Reddman. When I told him what had happened to me after he dropped me off, he grunted and opined it served me right. He'd always believed in justice, he said, and it didn't matter that I got punished for the wrong crime. I asked him if he'd realized I'd locked myself out, and he said the thought had occurred to him, but because I was a lawyer and all, he'd dismissed it. Then he laughed. I laughed too to show him I was a good fellow and we agreed to meet at Saliman's for a drink. After that I went to bed.

He may still be there, although I doubt it.

13

There are good and sufficient reasons for getting up early in the mountains. Tiny bubbles of dew will have formed on the grass; the sky is usually as clean and clear as the void between here and the moon. You feel like getting the wood in, so to speak, before an afternoon thunderstorm gets it all wet. Besides, everything else is already awake; it's expected of you, and with the sun in your eyes it's hard to sleep.

Most of these reasons don't exist in the city, where the focus is on the people to the exclusion of the rest of the forest. There isn't much grass in the first place and what's there is too short to catch the dew; the sky gets muddied even early by the thrashing and floundering of early risers; and no one gets up until he has to. In fact, with shades and pillows and brick walls to filter out the sun, generally you can manage to stay in the dark all day.

I'm one of those who adjusts very quickly to city routines. The next morning about eight thirty the blaring of a horn and the equally asinine retaliation of another one woke me up. A pillow had been over my face, muffling out most of it, like wearing a veil in hell; and my bed was soaked in sweat. I'd slept hard and it felt good, lying there, feeling drugged. Getting up was a struggle, but taking an ice-cold shower was pure joy.

The euphoric little interval didn't last, naturally. An article in the morning paper blew it apart. Referring to the customary "authoritative sources," this one also reported on the possibility that Watt Chambers had been hired to murder Cora Shannon. But it added a stroke the evening paper had missed, by suggesting that the person who did the hiring was Phillip Garver.

The men were known to have been acquainted, the report stated. They'd worked together on a political campaign less than a year ago. And a startling fact had developed out of the police investigation. It now appeared the black man had been killed with a weapon, purchased some weeks before, by Phillip Garver.

The small-caliber pistol had been found in the front seat of Chambers's car, near his body. In tracing the gun through its serial number, police found it had been sold to one Gavin Phillips. The mysterious Phillips (who could not be located) had sent a typewritten letter to Mason Brothers Sporting Goods, along with a postal money order for the price of the gun. The typewriter and paper had been identified as coming from the offices of Clear Sky—and Clear Sky was the environmentalist-action group administered by Phillip Garver.

Garver, who had bailed out of jail, could not be located for comment. It was believed the authorities were looking for him in order to serve him with a warrant for the murder of Chambers.

I read the article twice, but couldn't change it. The thing tired me out. I had no desire to spend the morning fighting Rollander, but now there was no choice.

He was an interesting mix of righteous indignation and white knight when I found him in his office, as though he'd just slain a dragon and still felt the thrill of combat. In a way, I felt sorry for him. The juices that moved him around were still in line with his life, and I wondered what

125

would happen when they betrayed him. "Quite an article in this morning's paper," I said.

"Where the hell is Garver, Tree?"

"Why? You serious about that murder warrant?"

"There may not be enough evidence for that, but there sure as hell is enough to raise his bail another hundred thousand dollars."

I showed him the note Garver had left me. "That's all I know."

"In other words, you've lost touch with your client?"

"I wasn't in touch with him in the first place. He just left."

Rollander grunted.

"You have a very distinct style, young man," I said. "I'd have laid in the woods."

"What the hell are you talking about?"

"I wouldn't have leaked that story in this morning's paper. Chances are, if you hadn't done that, you'd have surprised me with all this at the trial and I might even have lost the case." His mustache moved rhythmically as he gritted his teeth. "I need to see all your evidence, Peter. Everything you have."

He stared at me a full minute, then picked up the telephone and dialed a number. He's learning, I thought. "Lish? Nathan Tree is here . . . Yeah, I know, you'll have to let him . . . No argument, Lish. Everything . . ." He put his hand on the receiver. "When?" he asked me.

"Now."

"Ten minutes, Lish . . . Yeah, that too, if he asks for it . . . Don't I know." He hung up.

Not a bad kid, I thought, in spite of the water between his ears. "We used to have a tradition when I was here," I said, getting out of the chair. "After a trial, the lawyers'd go have a drink." He didn't look very interested. "It was a good thing to do," I went on. "The loser had to buy the winner a drink, and putting a trial in the context of a game smoothed over ruffled feelings. They still do that?"

"No."

"Just as well," I said. "The last time I had to buy, I got in a fist fight."

"Now *that* has possibilities," he said.

Lish's thick gray hair looked like a brush, and his stomach hung over his belt. He watched me walk down the hall of the police building with an expression of loathing, as though he was a member of the John Birch Society and I was in league with the Reds. "Sergeant," I said.

"You Nathan Tree?"

"That's right."

"Got some ID?"

I showed him my driver's license.

He had more keys on his ring than the head janitor and when we were in the basement he fingered one of them and let us into the evidence locker. It had tripled in size since I was in office, although the arrangement was basically the same. Rows and rows of heavy metal bookcases made aisles out of a large, open warehouse-sized room, and on the shelves were cardboard boxes of varying sizes filled with everything imaginable. It looked like the storeroom for a rummage sale. "What do you want to see first, Mr. Tree, sir?"

"The Watt Chambers exhibits."

He marched stoically to a card index file and pulled a card. "All over hell, sir. Come on."

We stopped at a bookcase numbered "186." He pulled a box off the top shelf and marched with it to the nearest wall, along which were spaced small tables. He put the box on a table and started carefully to unload it. "Clothing and personal effects," he said.

"This what he had on when he was shot?"

"It's what he had on when we found him, anyway."

I made the motions of going through the stuff. Chambers apparently had been wearing a dark-green turtleneck shirt, dark-blue trousers, and black suede shoes with spongy rubber soles. The only colorful item was his

127

shorts, which were silk or satin and cut out of a gaudy flower print. Lish picked up the shorts. "Guess he liked to keep his balls warm, sir."

"Anything in his pockets?"

"In that bag," he said, pointing.

I saw it and opened it. A billfold, some keys, and a Swiss Army knife were inside, as well as two rings and a wrist-watch. "Anything in the billfold?" I asked.

"Two fifty-dollar bills. No ID." His attitude toward me seemed to have softened, and I thought he might say something more. I let the silence grow. "He was out on a kill, travelin' light."

"Why the Swiss Army knife?"

"One of the best burglar tools there is, and no law against carryin' one, either."

"Anything more on Chambers?"

Carefully he repackaged the box, put it back, and consulted the card. "Come on," he said, leading the way to another bookcase.

This time the box he pulled off the shelf was small and specially constructed to hold up to three pistols, with slugs, casings, and photographs. Lish spread the contents on another table. "A twenty-five-caliber short-barrel Colt," he said, unwrapping a treated cloth from the weapon and handing it to me. "Brand new." It couldn't have been more than four inches long, and didn't look big enough to kill a prairie dog, let alone a man. "Found it in Chambers's car. Stuck between the seat and the door on the passenger side."

"Kind of obvious to leave the gun, isn't it?"

Lish shrugged. "When you kill a man, you don't always perform according to plan."

"What do you think happened, Sergeant?"

"You want to know, huh? Well, the way I see it, Garver and Chambers'd finished off that Shannon broad, drove off in Chambers's car. Garver pulled this gun on Watt-baby, had him pull over to the side of the street, got out. Leaned in through the open window and pow! Right in the temple. It killed Chambers and probably scared the crap out of Garver." He smiled as he thought about it. "Bet that college boy thought this little toy'd sound like a pea shooter. But you shoot off a firecracker in an echo chamber, it'll sound like a cannon. The way I see it, the explosion scared Garver so bad he dropped the gun and ran." He picked up the gun. "We ever find Garver's shorts, I think it'll prove my theory."

Some slugs were in small, sealed clear plastic bags, labeled and coded to conform to the photographs. "Did you conduct the ballistics tests?" I asked.

"Me personally? No."

"Any doubt about them?"

"Nope. Got a good make on the bullet in Chambers's head. A little lower he'd've hit the jawbone, might have flattened the lead, but the bone over the temple is thin and Chambers might as well've had feathers for brains, anyway."

"No question then that this is the gun he was killed with?"

"None."

"Fingerprints?"

"Nope. Garver was probably wearing gloves."

I looked at the trigger guard on the small Colt. "Could he have?"

"Gloves, Mr. Tree. Not ski mittens. You can get rubber gloves as thin as a toy balloon."

"Chambers wasn't wearing gloves though, was he?"

Lish shook his head. "Don't quite figure, either. Dark clothes, lightweight rubber-soled shoes, money, and a Swiss Army knife. That's Mack the Knife. He should've had gloves."

"You wouldn't consider the possibility that the person who shot him told him not to wear any, would you? So Chambers would have a chance to leave fingerprints in Garver's apartment?"

Lish laughed. "You defense lawyers are something," he said. "No, I don't think that and neither do you. This clown wasn't a super-cool professional Hawaii Five-O invention. Just a spade, earning pin money, who forgot his goddam gloves."

"Wasn't there a note in the car?"

"Yeah." He packaged the gun, slugs, and photographs, put them away, and we walked to another bookcase. "Here," he said, handing me two manila envelopes and then hefting an electric typewriter off the shelf. "We got to take it over there," he said, indicating with his head. "Only wall that has any outlets."

He set it down—an Olivetti Praxis—and plugged it in. Then he opened the envelopes and spread the documents over the table. Encased in plastic, with tape at the bottom covered with initials, was a small four- by six-inch sheet of white paper, discolored, I supposed, by chemical tests. Four words cut from newspapers or magazines were pasted on the paper: "Death to the Infidel."

I picked it up. "Have you made the words?"

"'Death,' 'to' and 'the' from the *Chronicle*. 'Infidel' we haven't found, the period we never will."

"What about the paper and glue?"

"Glue, LePage's household. Paper, Xerox copy. We found some where Garver works, by the way."

"The Clear Sky office? I don't remember a Xerox machine."

"They had some paper though. That lady stud—Barney Madden or whatever her name was—said they use the Xerox down the hall." He snorted. "Hell. The way those people are, they probably carry copy paper around so if they see some state secrets or some goddam thing they can steal them."

"Can you let me have a copy of the note?"

"Sure, if you have a dime. There's a photocopier over there." I started off. "Wait a minute." He picked another plastic-encased paper off the table and handed it to me. "Might as well get a copy of that too."

"What is it?"

"The letter Gavin Phillips wrote to Mason Brothers. On this typewriter."

"The typewriter is from the Clear Sky office?"

"That's right."

I made two copies of each document. When I got back Lish had cranked a sheet of paper into the machine and typed: "My name is Yon Yonson I come from Wisconsin."

"That for me?" I asked.

"Yeah. Paper's twenty-weight bond, like the letter from Gavin Phillips. We got some extra sheets."

"If it's all right with you, I'll type the letter."

"Go ahead."

I started typing: "Dear Sir. I am sending you inside this letter a money order for $64.87. Would you please send me the .25 Colt Automatic with the short barrel I seen in your mail order catalog? I work on a farm up here in Parker and cant get in. Send it to me, General Delivery, Parker, Colorado. Signed, Gavin Phillips."

"He even typed his signature," Lish said when I was done.

"What did Mason Brothers do with the letter?"

"Wrote to Phillips, told him they couldn't send the gun through the mail, but that they'd hold the money order and he could come in and pick it up."

"Did he?"

"Somebody did." He pulled a notebook out of his pocket and thumbed through it. "The clerk didn't ask for any ID, which he was supposed to do but nobody does. Naturally, the clerk don't remember a damn thing. All the law requires is for the purchaser to put down his name and address, which Gavin Phillips did."

"Enough for a handwriting sample?"

"Worried, counsel?" He found another sheet of paper,

131

packaged in plastic. "Printed it with his left hand, probably. Couldn't make that in a thousand years."

"So you think Garver picked up the pistol and disguised his writing?"

"Hell, yes, that's what I think."

"If somebody set him up, wouldn't they disguise their writing too? So everyone could go on thinking it was Garver?"

He laughed. "You guys never quit," he said, putting the stuff away. "That's all we got on Chambers. Anything else?"

"Show me what you took out of Garver's apartment."

He brought me to another bookcase. The middle shelf held three large cardboard boxes. "There it is," he said. "You can go ahead and go through it."

"All of that? What is it?"

"Clothes, mostly, belonging to the Shannon girl."

"Anything else?"

"Perfumes, bath powders, face creams, jewelry."

I looked inside the boxes, touching the things she'd worn, trying to get to know her possibly, but not wanting to get very close. "You have an inventory?"

"Yeah." It was inside an envelope taped to the side of the middle box.

"I'd like some copies, but I'm out of dimes," I said.

He dug into his pocket. "You defense lawyers are all alike."

After making the copies I came back, studying the pages. "No mail, personal papers, checkbook, identification—not even a purse or a billfold. Didn't you take any of that?"

"None of it there to take. We figure Garver tossed all that stuff out."

"Then told me what her real name was? Why?"

"Don't ask me." He had started putting the boxes back on the shelf. "Want to see anything else?"

"There's nothing else to see, is there?"

"Nope." He grinned at me as he let me out the door. "Riggs says you were one helluva DA."

"Good old Cousin Charlie," I said.

I telephoned Garver's father from my office and arranged to see the old man in an hour. Before he'd retired from politics, and back in the days when the Burning Issues of the Day were on my mind, we had met. We had not gotten along, of course. For one thing, he was a Liberal and, for another, I was a Bigot. It used to be hard for me to talk to a man with a different religion.

I finished my beer, put on a clean shirt, and went outside. It had gotten cooler. High white clouds had built up around Long's Peak, but they hadn't closed out the sun, and the sight of them soaking in the deep blue sky was as restful as staring at a campfire. It started me thinking about my ranch, and I drove to the parkway along Cherry Creek, where I got out and sat on the grass. A squirrel came partway down the trunk of a cottonwood tree and we examined each other a moment or two, until a long-haired young giant strode between us. He had on one of those mountaineer's hats, mass-produced out of plastic leather, high-ridge Kletter boots, and a brand-new orange backpack. For camping in City Park, I thought. His gaze swept the mountain vista to the west as though he were Jeremiah Johnson on his way back home, and I wondered what would happen if he tried to walk over them.

Later I drove toward Senator Garver's home. He lived in an area called the Polo Grounds, and at one time that was what they were. In the 1880's some wealthy Denver citizens decided to live like lords and ladies, so they carved a polo grounds out of the prairie in order to give their fantasies some substance. Now their descendants lived in elegant homes where the old nobles used to play. Maybe they weren't so different from the mountain man I'd just seen on Cherry Creek, I thought. The fantasies were different, but each generation ought to be entitled to its own insanity. Senator Garver's place settled in the back of a rolling, landscaped three-acre estate like an old English manor, high enough to see most of the Front Range but too low to see Pike's Peak.

The Senator, a large man with a deep tan and silver hair, tried to smile when he saw me but couldn't. His wife, whom I had never met except for the disaster in the courtroom, tried too. She had even less success. She was small, nervous, and still pretty—at least fifteen years younger than the old man—and I saw where Phillip had gotten his black hair and firm face.

At one time it would have surprised me to find that Liberals, especially rich ones, can be nice, decent people. It doesn't any more, however. Nothing does. I found I liked them both. The old man said he had the impression I might be a drinking man, but after watching me perform in court he knew it couldn't be true. He was nice about it. He even offered me a drink, which I took, and then toasted my good health.

They didn't know any more than I did as to the whereabouts of their son. He'd talked to his mother just before leaving—most of his camping gear was stored with them—and he'd taken enough to be out a couple of weeks. He told her he planned to stay away as long as he could, but even if he smelled like a mule, he'd be back for the preliminary.

When I asked for a set of keys to Phillip's apartment, they looked at each other and didn't move. I told them I wanted to search it, on the off chance the police had missed something. Mrs. Garver left to get them, and while she was gone the Senator said he didn't want to question my judgment, but he understood I was having his daughter-in-law followed and wondered if that were necessary. I hemmed and hawed until his wife got back, then changed the subject. She gave me the keys, and as I left I promised to keep in touch.

Oddly enough, the Garver family reminded me of my

134

own. More money possibly and a different political bent, but my father—who called himself a frontier banker even though he missed the early days by forty years—had been every bit as proud as the Senator, and twice as tough. His were the days when a family took pride in its name, and when I quit my campaign for High Public Office, it killed him.

Or so I thought at the time, anyway. Now I'm not so sure. He may have just been ready to die, and used that for an excuse.

Hunter's secretary got up as I entered the RMBI building and ushered me into her boss's office. She seemed embarrassed about something; on an impulse I winked, to show her I wasn't such an old shit, but it didn't do any good. She still looked embarrassed.

The afternoon paper was on his desk. "You read this?" he asked. "Gavin Phillips and Phillip Garver?"

"I read it."

"You think you'll ever see him again? Garver, I mean?"

"See if you can find him," I said, "before he gets his fanny in a bigger crack than it's already in." Then I told him about my tour of the evidence locker and gave him copies of everything I'd photostated. "Can you check this stuff out?" He nodded. "Anything new on Sharon?"

"Well . . . Don't ask me how I found out, okay?" I sat down. "A new agent—new to me, been in the game fifteen years—last night his assignment was Sharon Garver. Seems he overheard a discussion between Sharon and her husband."

"Oh?"

"Husband Pete accused wife of hanky-pank with brother Phil."

"Did it get violent?"

"No sir. Tears and promises, both sides."

"Did he tell her how he knew?"

135

"No sir."

"Get that bug the hell out of their bedroom. Anything else?"

"No, Mr. Tree."

I gave him the keys to Garver's apartment and asked him to search it as soon as he could. Some things that belonged to the Shannon girl were missing—her purse, and personal papers. Shouldn't there be some correspondence, or professional journals, or something? Hunter agreed. She was a professional geologist. They carry attache cases with them everywhere—even on vacations —although he didn't think they ever opened them.

I got up. "Can you get a subpoena out this afternoon and serve it for me?"

"Sure can. Who?"

"Sharon. The preliminary's July twenty-eighth, and I want her there."

"You're going to put on evidence at a preliminary?"

"I don't know. But if she thinks she has to testify, she might also think we know a lot more than we do."

He looked worried. "The guy who stole the cassette will think so too. You trying to get her killed?"

"Not that I know of," I said.

Peter Garver was easy to find. I telephoned first—he was "most anxious to meet me"—and then drove to the college. I found his office in one of the modern prefabricated buildings that clutter the campus.

He looked like the All-American Boy, with sandy hair and freckles and blue eyes set wide above a pug nose. When we shook hands he said "Hi," grinning with the ingenuous warmth of the boy next door. He wasn't as tall as his brother, but he had the same healthy glow, as though he had spent the afternoon playing touch football.

Witches such as Sharon are often attracted to the type, I thought. They like to work their magic on the souls of such

136

men. They take special pleasure in mashing their façades into jelly.

"These latest reports in the papers, Mr. Tree. Don't they kind of change things?" he asked me.

"In what way?"

"Listen. You don't have to beat around the bush." He regarded me with satisfaction. "I can take it, Mr. Tree. I may not like it, but I can take it."

I had a sudden feeling about Peter. He probably had to fight his younger brother's fights when they were growing up and later had to endure his fame. Now his brother had made a cuckold of him. Taken all together, it must be quite a maturing experience. "Are you trying to tell me you think he killed her?"

"Not just her. Watt Chambers too."

"How well do you know your brother?"

"I thought I knew him pretty well, but I'm not so sure any more."

Sometimes I wonder if the truth is worth it. Sometimes I think, "Timothy, leave me alone."

"What did you say?" he asked me.

"Nothing. How long have you known about the two of them?"

"The two of who?"

"Phillip and Sharon."

"What the hell are you talking about, Tree?"

"Your wife and your brother," I said. "Their little affair."

"That's a lie. A dirty, rotten lie."

"Is it?"

His face turned red and his eyes filmed over with some kind of harsh veneer. "You've been having her followed, haven't you?" he shouted. "Who the hell do you think you are, Tree? God Almighty?"

"She knew something was in that waterbed. What about you, Peter? What did you know?"

"Get out, Tree, goddam you. Get out."

137

I telephoned Hunter from a phone booth on the campus, and as we talked I watched the girls go by. Some of them strode with militant purpose, as though the world depended on their mission, whatever it was. Others skylarked along like playful otters. But they were different from the ones I used to know, I thought. Now they have thin lips.

"Sharon's been served, Mr. Tree," Hunter said. "She didn't like it, either." The mountains in the distance were purple, which is the way they get when the late afternoon sun turns their surfaces into shadow. "She's getting hard to cover, too. If she really wants to lose us, ain't no way we can stop her."

I was tired. I wished the son of a bitch would kill her so I wouldn't have to worry about keeping her alive. "Use teams," I said.

"That gets very expensive, Mr. Tree."

"I know it does," I said, and hung up.

Then I tried to drive back to my office, but my truck wouldn't go that way. It takes over now and then, like a stable horse at a dude ranch that decides the ride has been long enough. She stopped for gas, then headed for the hills.

The night was fine. A thin moon dropped toward the pale-blue horizon and overhead the Milky Way, like the exhaust from a huge white comet, seemed to settle into the deep-blue void. Toward ten I turned right out of Elk Park and after fifteen minutes on a dirt road, I left it for the ruts that trail up Shadow Mountain. My place is in a swale on the other side. The aspen by the creek are so big you can't reach around them, and the mosquitoes in the summer will keep you from trying. I parked in the shed and wandered toward the house, soaking in the quiet, brilliant night.

"That you, Gringo?" Danny said as I came through the door and turned on the light. He was listening to the radio in the kitchen as he tooled a design on a piece of leather

138

stretched over a board. "Some three-day coffee on the stove, if you want to stay awake the rest of your life."

Danny's an ex-convict who found his wife making love to a friend. He beat them badly and managed to kill the man. Now he's blind, although the doctors can't find anything wrong with his eyes. He feels things more intensely than most of us and crowds it into the agonized faces he embosses in wall-size patches of leather. They are generally faces of Christ, or studies of Judas, but from a distance you could mistake them for Indians.

He keeps the fires warm when I'm in town.

14

The eastern sky had started to lighten with the false dawn. There were deer in the meadow below me: I could hear them grazing by the creek. Now and then one would skit up the wooded hill on the other side, or splash softly through the water.

I was stretched out on a large granite boulder that jutted out of the hill north of the meadow, soaking in the stillness and hoping the breeze wouldn't blow across me toward the deer. They'd pick up my scent and leave before it was light, and for some reason I wanted to see them.

Slowly, the rolling outline of the mountain behind the meadow began to separate from the lightening sky. The tall spruce in the corner grew more and more distinct, so magnificent in their dignity, and as the first pink light hit the mountaintop I could see the deer in the shelter of the pine.

It was Monday morning, the twentieth of July, and I'd been at my ranch since Friday night. I had to get back to Denver, with its straight lines and asphalt paths, but couldn't make myself move. The deer in the meadow held me there. I've known people with gentle smells who can get close enough to touch them, but I'm not one of those people. My younger brother had been, though. Then one fall I persuaded him to hunt with me, and after that he lost it.

I thought about the kid. He'd been bucked off a motorcycle at the age of thirty-three, ending a wild search for who knows what?—maybe to regain the gentle smell. I got to my feet. From the point of view of the deer it must have looked as though the top of the rock had lifted off, and I could hear them crash through the brush, racing up the mountain behind them.

Peculiar, I suppose, the way one thought will lead to another. The girl I'd always known I would marry was at the funeral too. Her hair was as black as it had been in college and her skin held the same vibrant quality—like a movie princess—and she radiated that wacky humor and same soft assurance. Life as the wife of a Rising Young Politician struck her as dull, however, so she married the son of a textile manufacturer in New England. He was an expert on ninth-century Chinese jade.

At the graveside service she held my father's arm, and it kind of propped him up. That was a nice thing for her to do. She held mine too and squeezed it, and I could still remember how good it felt.

"Hey, Gringo, how 'bout some eggs?" Danny asked, half an hour later as I walked inside. He sat in the kitchen working on the tortured face of Judas, and might not have moved from Friday night.

"I'll get them," I said. "They taste better without shells."

It took three hours to drive to Denver. North of town, over Commerce City, brown stains pooled in the sky like spilled ink, but the air over Denver was clear. As I dropped in from the mountains I could see groups of buildings scattered over the plain like toy blocks on the living room floor, throwing geometric shadows, as unreal and eerie as a mirage. The traffic built as I came toward town and the clang of it brought me back. Lord. I parked in front of my office and walked up the stairs, and learned from Hunter that Sharon was still alive.

My answering service told me Charlie Riggs had tried twice the night before to call. I reached him at his office just as he was coming in and he said he'd meet me for a breakfast steak at Coffee's, as long as he could count on me to buy it.

Half an hour later I watched as he poured catsup all over the steak, the potatoes, and the eggs. He cut off a large chunk of meat, speared it with his fork, then popped the yellow out of an egg and swirled the meat around. He shook it until a glob or two fell off, then crammed it in his mouth. "No wonder you're so skinny," he said. "Live in the mountains like a goddam nature boy. What'd you have for breakfast, Nathan? Sunflower seeds?"

"Careful. You'll make both of us sick."

"You been following that Gretchen Flanders thing?"

I'd heard something on the radio about her while watching Danny tool the face out of leather. "From Germany, wasn't she? Married to an Air Force sergeant?"

"Yeah. Two kids. Got herself strangled Saturday night while you was gone. Happened in an apartment she rented on Corona Street, turns out she hustled on the side."

"What about her?"

He held the fork in his hand, ready to jab another piece of meat. "The killer left a note. You hear about that?"

"No."

"You will," he said. "When the papers get it, we got a problem."

"Why?" Something in my forehead started to prickle.

"Looks like a ransom note. Know the kind? Words cut out of a newspaper or magazine, pasted on paper."

"What does it say?"

" 'One for the Father.' And the damnedest thing, know what it reminded me of?"

"Watt Chambers," I said. "The note with Chambers."

"How did you know that?"

142

My stomach started to roil with funny waves. Columbus might have felt the same thing, sailing toward the edge of the earth and wondering if he could be wrong. "Tell me about it."

Charlie wiped his plate with a piece of toast. "Just a hunch, Nathan, but I wanted you to know." He started sucking at a piece of meat between his teeth. "Saturday night, eleven or so, a patrol car answered a call at a small apartment house on Corona Street. The Arlington Arms. The manager wanted the officers to break in an apartment on the third floor because a tenant'd heard some strange sounds, seen some weirdo run out.

"So the officers went in, found this Flanders dame on the bed. Nothing on, except an imitation leopard-skin robe." He took some coffee. "Strangled pretty good, too. Collapsed the trachea, even broke those little hyoid bones in the neck." He spoke comfortably and offered me a cigar, which I refused. "We figure the guy is a nut."

"Why?"

"Mainly because of the note." He lit the cigar. "An efficient bastard, though. Strangled her quick, then laid that note on her navel where you couldn't really miss it, then got the hell away." His eyes stopped on my toast. "You gonna eat all that?"

"No."

He laid on the marmalade, then held the toast in his hand, ready to push it in his mouth. "Just for the hell of it, I compared the note on her navel with the one we found by Chambers. A funny thing. They kind of look alike."

"How?"

"Different paper, different glue, different magazines. All the obvious stuff is different." The toast went in, but he didn't seem to notice it. "It's the way the words are put on the paper that's kind of the same." He took a ball-point pen and found a clean napkin. "Like this," he said, drawing. " 'Death to the Infidel.' See, the words 'Death' and

143

'Infidel' are set out, like they were underlined. Same with the words 'One' and 'Father.'"

"Show me the notes."

"I don't know, Nathan. Rollander finds out, I've had it." Then he shrugged, patted his mouth with his napkin, and struggled to his feet. "What the hell. I got seniority." I picked up the ticket. "Can't hurt anyway. There can't be a connection."

I paid the bill and pushed him out the door. "Did you get a description?"

"Yeah. Huge. Seven feet tall," he said, working a toothpick in his mouth. "Disguised, too. We found part of a false mustache on the floor."

A few minutes later we were inside the police building, walking down the basement hallway toward the evidence locker. "'One for the Father.' What's he saying?"

The large man flipped through the wad of keys in his hand and made a selection. "'One for the money, two for the show'—remember?—'three to get ready, four to go.' That's what's got us worried."

"You're expecting more killings?"

"The papers will be. Bet your ass on that."

He found the notes and brought them to one of the tables along the wall. When I had them side by side, the hollow feeling in my chest started to swell. "It's like handwriting, Charlie. The same person wrote them both."

"I don't see it," he said, lying like hell.

I compared them, point by point. "Death" and "Infidel" were capitalized, "to" and "the" were not; "One" and "Father" were capitalized, "for" and "the" were not. Both notes were punctuated—"Death to the Infidel" with a period, "One for the Father" with a comma. I pointed all this out to him, but didn't need to. He could read. "That comma. A little ominous, wouldn't you say?"

"The trouble is . . ."

"Don't kid yourself. Even the phrases are alike. The

144

same symmetry, the same sing-song pattern. This is more than a hunch and you know it."

"A lot less than proof, and I know that, too." He glared at them. "Sure they look alike. So what? How you gonna make notes like that so they *don't* look alike? Besides, everything else is different. Chambers got shot in the temple in his car. Flanders got herself strangled on a bed. One is an execution, pure and simple. The other is the work of an insane son of a bitch."

"Pure and simple."

"What do you mean?"

My stomach felt as though someone had dumped garbage down my throat. "Remember the old days, how easy it was to prove *modus operandi?*"

"Yeah. You'd convince the jury the defendant signed his goddam name to the crime. You'd compare the one he was charged with to some others he'd committed, convince everybody they were done by the same man."

"We pushed background, remember? The accumulation of all the obvious similarities, so obvious you don't even see them?"

"Yeah. Well, what's similar here, except they're both dead? Hell. So's Cora Shannon."

My body had grown cold, as though I'd been standing in a freezer. "They look alike to me," I said. "Cora Shannon, Watt Chambers, Gretchen Flanders."

"Alike? One planted in a waterbed, another shot in the head, the third one strangled. What the hell's alike about that?"

"The same flair, Charlie. The same notorious flair. And look at the motive. Garver knocks up a lady, so he kills her. Chambers—first the obvious motive, executed by black fanatics—now just as obviously murdered by Garver. And Flanders, obviously murdered by a nut."

"What the hell are you getting at?"

"Each time, the motive is so goddam obvious."

He laughed. "That's background?"

It had started, and unless I could turn it around, it would end with Sharon. "Right," I said. "That's background."

The Arlington Arms was a three-story blond brick building with a neatly kept lawn and benches along the sidewalk. I thought it would be surrounded by rubberneckers, but the people moving by didn't even glance at it. I hurried up the steps and rang for the manager.

A middle-aged man wearing a sport shirt, cotton trousers, and a suspicious expression came up to the landing from carpeted steps that disappeared into the basement. "Are you the manager?" I finally asked.

"Yes."

"I'd like some information on Gretchen Flanders."

"Who are you?"

I took ten dollars out of my billfold. "A lawyer. This won't take long."

"Will it get me in trouble?" he asked, reaching for the money.

"No." He put the bill in his pocket. "Can you show me the apartment?"

"Don't see why not. I even rented it this morning. The new tenants haven't moved in yet, though." He led the way up the stairs. "Thought I'd have trouble, but I had another vacancy and got it rented, too."

"Nothing like a little publicity."

"Number Three A," he said, when we were on the third floor. "Always did think it was too quiet in there. Never even saw her except once, twice a week, usually about eight. Most of the time a man'd go up with her, stay until ten or eleven, then leave."

"Would you recognize them?"

"Not 'them,' mister. Him. Always the same guy."

"Who was he?"

"Lester A. Dodson," he said, fitting a key in the lock. "Cops showed me his picture and I heard them talking."

146

"Do they think he did it?"

"Way I get it, they think he paid the rent, but they don't think he killed her." A drape over the large front window was open, lighting up the room, and it seemed to emphasize the bed. It was covered with a bright quilt and jutted out from the wall like a pillar that had fallen over. "A hooker, I guess," the man said, "but neat as a pin. Didn't even have to vacuum the rug. I tried to give the cleanup deposit back to hubby, but he wouldn't take it."

"When was he here?"

"Saturday night to identify the body, then yesterday to get her stuff. You should've seen him."

I was glad I hadn't. "Did you see the so-called maniac that did it?"

"No. The lady in Three C did, though."

"She there now?"

"Maybe, mister, but I don't want to bother her."

I judged the gleam in his eye to be worth about five dollars, and took out another bill. "Just introduce us. Tell her it's all right."

"I don't even know your name," he said, taking the money.

"Make one up."

We walked down the hall and I thought I saw the door to Three C move. "Mrs. Lilte told me the creep almost knocked her down," the manager said, raising his hand to knock and then realizing the door was ajar. "Mrs. Lilte?"

The door opened and a tall, thin woman in her sixties stood there. She was dressed nicely, as though expecting company. "Good morning, Mr. Surlton," she said, but her bright eyes examined me as they would a long-lost son. "Won't you gentlemen come in?"

"I can't, Mrs. Lilte. Like you to meet . . ."

"He really needs no introduction." She held her hand out grandly and I took it. "I'd recognize you anywhere, Mr. Tree. I was on one of your juries—that Pettersenn case —but I don't suppose you remember *me*."

"No."

"Of course not. But you did such a wonderful job. And I must confess, I had a doubt. It simply wasn't a *reasonable* doubt, and you told us it had to be reasonable before we could let it affect our judgment." I must have looked interested because she kept on talking. "That gardener, remember, the one who testified to buying all the materials for the son? I always sort of thought *he* was the one, but couldn't decide why. Isn't that odd?" She took my arm. "Please. Won't you come in?"

The manager grinned and walked away and I forced myself through her door. My voice sounded as though it were coming in through a window. "I understand you saw the man who killed Mrs. Flanders."

"Quite a desperate-looking man, Mr. Tree." She continued to cling to my arm, as though to tell me now she felt safe.

"Can you describe him?"

"Actually I didn't see him very well. I just happened to be standing in the hallway when he came *bursting* out of that poor girl's apartment." She tossed her hands in the air and before she could grab me, I backed up. "He was *huge*, Mr. Tree. Even taller than you. And when he saw me he actually growled—" she hunched over and made claws of her hands, like an Indian pretending to be a grizzly bear— "and stalked after me as though I were his prey! Quite mad, I should say." It obviously delighted her to have something of such importance to talk about. "Of course he had on only half a mustache, which added to his disordered expression—and dark glasses, and a hat. Without them, as I told the police, I should never be able to recognize him. I simply couldn't."

"What were you doing in the hall, Mrs. Lilte?"

"Oh," she said. "Well. I heard a noise, you see, and stepped into the hallway." Her large eyes seemed to plead with me for understanding.

"You heard a noise. Then your door was open?"

"As a matter of fact, it was. Just a little. Saturday night was really quite warm."

"Did you see him come up the stairs?"

"Oh, no. But I must confess, Mr. Tree, that I heard him. He even talked to her for a moment before going into the apartment."

"What did he say?"

"Just that it was nice to see her and could he come in."

"Do you remember his words, Mrs. Lilte?"

Her mouth worked quietly for a moment and then stopped. "I'm sorry." Then she put her hand on my arm and stared at me. "But I can remember the way he sounded, Mr. Tree."

"How did he sound?"

"Like such a nice man." A measure of compassion seemed to have infected the woman's tone. "I'm a foolish old busybody, Mr. Tree—a snoop—I expect *that* is plain enough. But at first I thought he was just a lonely man, perhaps, whose wife—I read quite a lot, Mr. Tree. But then those frightful sounds came from the room—he couldn't have been inside more than two minutes—and his expression when he left . . . He can't *possibly* have intended to do what he did."

The hell he didn't, I thought. Unless he took magazines, scissors, and glue in there with him and made up the note after he killed her. "What was he wearing?"

"An old coat—quite disreputable-looking, actually—and black baggy trousers."

"Gloves?"

"Yes. White, and they seemed to fit his hands very tightly."

"On his feet?"

"Boots. Those Arctic-looking things, made of rubber, with the tops of his trousers tucked inside."

"Do you know Lester Dodson, Mrs. Lilte?"

"I've never actually met him, although the police showed me his picture. It definitely was not Mr. Dodson."

149

"Did you ever see the girl with anyone other than Dodson?"

"I am a snoop, Mr. Tree, but I don't often open the door far enough to actually see what is going on." She smiled. "I'm a *timid* snoop. But I did manage on two occasions to step into the hallway as a man was leaving that poor girl's apartment, and once it was Mr. Dodson, and once another man."

"The other man. Could it have been him?"

"No. It . . ."

"Thank you, Mrs. Lilte," I said, opening the door and hurrying into the hall. It surprised both of us.

"Oh! Would you . . ."

"No. But thank you."

I started to run from there. Timothy Pettersenn's shit-eating grin seemed to float out there on a balloon. My hands were numb, and when I looked at them they were white.

15

There are different ways to drink, just as there are different ways to eat steak. It depends on your objective. Sometimes, for example, I like catsup on my steak. It tastes better with lots of catsup in expensive restaurants, where the wine is vintage French and the waiters manage to look horrified if you pick your nose; and I am just as flexible when it comes to drinking. I don't always slug down whisky as fast as I can in a wild race with my mind to wipe out. Sometimes I drink beer—enough to keep my mind quiet—and have found I can live on it for days.

That afternoon, I started drinking beer. My memory with respect to the next few days isn't indelibly sharp— some details may have slipped away and I am not certain of the order—but the high points stayed in my mind. William Drake called to tell me he'd given the copy of the memorandum I'd given him to Dix, and not long after that, I heard from the old man himself. "I can add as well as any man," he said, "and I recognize I am in your debt. Don't know why you did it, Tree, or how, but I no sooner tell you there has to be another report than I get one." I tried to tell him I didn't know what he was talking about, but in an exuberant voice he said he knew better. "Do you know, Tree, I even hope you get that young radical off.

You must have stirred up quite a hornet's nest. It occurs to me your father might not have been as mule-headed as I thought!"

Later that day I took a call from Gerry Ashe.

Gerry has a reputation as one of the best criminal lawyers in the state, and I like to think he owes it to me. I once prosecuted a man who killed his neighbor by shooting him five times in the stomach, in front of witnesses, and Gerry defended. The jury chose to acquit. I hadn't liked the fat, bald-headed little screamer before the trial began, and found I liked him a whole lot less when it was over.

He'd been hired by Sharon Garver, he told me. She wanted him to do something about that ridiculous subpoena she'd been served with. Gerry asked me as a friend not to enforce the goddam thing. His client didn't want to go to Phillip's preliminary hearing, she'd told him; none of her friends believed in his innocence, now that everyone knew he'd murdered Watt Chambers too; it would be a funeral and she hated funerals. Besides, she and her husband had tickets to Hawaii and they simply were not going to be in town.

The trip to Hawaii interested me and I questioned Gerry about it. He admitted the opportunity had come up suddenly, and they weren't going to leave until the day before the hearing. I thought I recognized the pattern, which I'd seen more than once in the DA's office. She'd been bought. "Sorry I can't help you, old friend," I told him. "She'll have to be there."

Gerry threw his usual tantrum after that. He threatened me with a million-dollar lawsuit, for defaming his client by suggesting an affair between her and Garver, and for harassment by having her followed. I asked him to go ahead and sue because the publicity should help my case. "You've had it with me, Tree!" he shouted, and hung up.

It was either that day or the next that Hunter gave me a report on Lester Dodson.

The police found a bathrobe in Flanders's apartment,

and in a pocket was a letter addressed to Dodson. Their investigation showed she was mainly his mistress, although she'd developed a brisk little trade on the side. Dodson apparently was in love, and didn't know about the business transactions that didn't involve him—which ordinarily would have qualified him as a suspect, except that two days before her death he'd flown from Denver to the Andes on a ski vacation.

Then Tuesday afternoon I got a telephone call from Riggs. His voice sounded like a tight wire, and I thought it was too bad Charlie's habits didn't allow for a greater intake of beer. "That comma in the note you said was ominous?"

"Yes."

"We got a make on the robe that Flanders broad had on. The Niwot Shop in Colorado Springs."

"Go on."

"The weirdo bought three robes."

"When?"

"Friday, July seventeenth. The day before he used the first one."

"What about a description?"

"It matches the one we got at the Arlington Arms. Big guy—six four or five—wild-looking. We got our artist working up a portrait."

"You already know it's a disguise," I said.

"Yeah."

Then on Tuesday night, the twenty-first of July, the "weirdo" dropped another robe.

I had coffee the next morning for breakfast, instead of beer. Riggs sat next to me on the sofa in my office. "Who is she?" I asked, trying not to see the picture in my hand. It showed a flabby white body, huddled on a rickety-looking brass bed like a little girl, waiting to be whipped. An imitation leopard-skin robe covered part of one leg.

"Name's Elizabeth Farre. Husband's the principal at

Mountview Junior High in South Denver." Charlie had deep circles under his eyes. "Been up the whole goddam night," he said, hunched over his coffee as though lighting a cigarette in the wind. I got up and poured some whisky in his cup. "I'd have called sooner," he said, "but I couldn't get away."

"Was there a note?"

"Yeah. Covered her navel, just like the other one. Says, 'One for the Son.'"

"Is it punctuated with a comma?"

"Yeah." He swallowed some coffee and made a face. "Jesus. Eight o'clock in the morning and I'm having my first drink."

I threw the mug in my hand across the room. It made a gentle sound when it splintered against the wall, like the cracking of glacial ice.

"What the hell did you do that for?" Charlie yelped.

"I felt like it."

He tried to keep his coffee from sloshing over the edge. "Crazy bastard," he said.

Suddenly my hands covered my face. I could feel fingers digging like nails into my head. "God damn me," I said. "God damn me."

Charlie's fingers gently pried at mine and he managed to pull my hands away from my face. "Hey," he said. "You act like it's your fault. It ain't your fault."

"Mmm."

"We got the guy anyway, Nathan."

"Who?"

"Part-time actor, works for Geisler Electric. Does their advertising and promotion, which means he draws a salary. His uncle owns it."

"What's his name?"

"Julian Thoms."

"What makes you so sure he's the one?"

Charlie held out his cup and I poured more whisky in, then took a swallow from the bottle and let it warm my throat. "His background, mainly. Frustrated actor, old man an Episcopal preacher who died of cirrhosis of the liver."

"Go on."

"'One for the Father, One for the Son'—and he buys three robes. We figure the third one was for the Holy Ghost."

"A very obvious nut. Right, Charlie?"

"Yeah." He looked thoughtful, which was rare for Charlie, and I was glad when it went away. "Religious freak with a mission. Strangle evil women."

"What have you got?"

He settled into the sofa and dug out a cigar. "Last night, eleven o'clock, we get a call from the Arena Hotel on Fourteenth Street. Know it? It'll be coming down soon, Urban Renewal." He sucked on the cigar as though it were a piece of candy, then stuck it in his mouth and lit it. "The TV in this particular room—Five Eleven—had been turned all the way up and the door was unlocked. Some cowboy in the next room stood the noise as long as he could, then stomped in there to give whoever it was a piece of his mind. That's what he saw." Charlie bent his head toward the picture I'd laid on my desk.

"Naturally, by the time we get there them hotel people have it solved. The name on the register is fictitious but the clerk says he'd recognize the guy anywhere. Seems he and Elizabeth been goin' to the same hotel, even gettin' the same room, sometimes two, sometimes three times a month."

"How did you get her identified?"

"Her purse. On the bureau. So we called her husband and he gave us the name of Julian Thoms."

"He knew?"

"Yeah. Not much of a secret." He puffed on the cigar until he'd covered himself with smoke, like a mountain shrouded in fog. "We get Julian's address and haul-ass over there. An apartment on Santa Fe Drive. Julian isn't

155

there but his roommate is—young guy, looks like one of them consenting adults—tells us Julian went out to dinner about eight. I stay, thinking he'll be back nice and innocent, and about twelve thirty he staggers in half drunk."

"And?"

"He admits he got the room at the Arena. We already had a picture ID of him from the clerk, so it wouldn't have done him any good to lie. Says he didn't kill her. Says some guy gave him two hundred dollars. Says the guy told him he was desperately in love with her, and Julian figured it was a good way to get her off his back, pick up a few bucks at the same time."

A daddy long-legs started across the rug and I thought about stepping on him, but didn't. "What happened after that?"

"We bring him in, book him, he acts surprised. It's a frame-up, he says. Elizabeth's husband must have set him up, then killed her."

"What about the husband? Could he have done it?"

"Nope. He was at a school board meeting. That's where we reached him. Julian is the one, Nathan. Dippy. Murdering wicked adulteresses, probably on instructions from God." He finished his coffee and started to stand. "What we need for proof is that third robe. He's got it hidden somewhere."

"Has he been identified by that shop in Colorado Springs?"

"Don't know yet and it won't mean much anyway. The guy's an actor."

"He can't very well fake his size, can he? Is Thoms six four?"

"He could be if he wore rubber boots. He could damn near wear stilts inside them boots and you couldn't tell it." He stretched and yawned, still not on his feet. "He's the one. Something'll click. We'll find out he was one of Gretchen's customers, maybe."

"Does he have a lawyer?"

156

"Why?"

"Thoms didn't kill her. Maybe his lawyer will let me talk to him."

Charlie looked thoughtful again, and I still didn't like it. "His lawyer's Mike Johns. Know him?"

"No."

"Young guy, nice enough, over his head on this one, though. Rollander'll chew him to pieces and spit out anything he can't swallow." He leaned forward so far that it forced him to stand. It was either that or roll away on the floor. "Thanks for the coffee. Hear anything from Garver?"

"No. Why?"

"Just wondering if he has a pair of rubber boots."

Mike Johns, Richard Hunter, and I waited in the small room until Julian Thoms was brought in and the handcuffs were taken off. There was something noble about the man. Although clad in simple prison clothes, he stared angrily around the room, as though cast in the role of a captured king. Then he nodded his magnificent head and sat down, indicating that now the war could begin.

"This is Mr. Tree, Julian. Mr. Nathan Tree," Mike Johns said. He was a tall, thin youngster who affected a professional stoop. "This other gentleman is Mr.—Hunter, did you say?"

"Right."

"They think they can help us. I want you to answer their questions. Do you understand me?"

"Really, Mike. You haven't said anything very complicated."

"I'll be here to—to protect your rights," Johns said, growing a little red.

"I doubt if *that* will be necessary." Thoms flashed a smile at me. "Please, Mr. Tree. Sit down."

I did, in the only other chair. "I understand you told the police you rented the . . ."

". . . room at the Arena Hotel? Yes I did. But not for

157

myself, Mr. Tree. For another man." He waggled that beautiful head. "You see, Elizabeth had grown rather—tiresome. That may seem rather callous of me but it's true, nevertheless."

"What did the man . . ."

"Look like? I have no idea. We handled the matter on the telephone."

I glanced at Johns, who shrugged. "That's part of the difficulty, Mr. Tree. The police don't believe it."

"Tell me about it. From the beginning," I said.

Julian pushed back into his chair. "I first met Elizabeth at—at a bowling alley." The recollection surprised him, as though he couldn't believe they had met in such a mundane place. "She recognized me, you see. I had played in a Shakespearean festival in Detroit and when we met, she actually asked for my autograph." He smiled. "She was quite an appealing woman, Mr. Tree. Mature, lonely, unfulfilled. Had you met her, Mike?"

"No."

"I thought not." He pronounced the words with care. "Frankly, I had no idea of her social prominence. Surprising really, that the wife of a junior high school principal should be socially prominent. But then Denver is quite different from Detroit."

I cleared my throat. "All right. When was the first time you slept with her?"

"We met in January, after the holidays, and it didn't take long at all." He delivered himself of a masculine smile. "I should say five months ago."

"Go on."

"Well. It grew rather—boring. We must always go to the same hotel, as though she could not feel passion in any other. And so for a period of, oh, three or four months, we had these rather regular engagements. However, as I said, it became rather tiresome. And then this last Saturday I received a telephone call from a man who told me he couldn't identify himself. I thought perhaps he might ac-

158

tually be Elizabeth's husband." A smile emanated from the actor's presence. "He made a perfectly outrageous proposal. He said he would pay me three hundred dollars for no more than the opportunity to meet her. Obviously, the fellow knew of our meetings. We had never been very discreet, I'm afraid. His proposal was that if I would arrange for the room as well as for Elizabeth's presence, then he would pay me the money—only *he* would meet her there, rather than me!"

He suppressed a small chuckle. "I know how perfectly awful it must seem, but at the time, it struck me as hilarious! Boccaccio couldn't have written a more charming tale. And to have seen Elizabeth's face when she first realized another man was in bed with her! Perhaps I'm a bit kinky, but it struck me as priceless."

"I saw a picture of her body," I said.

"Believe me, Mr. Tree, not for a *moment* did I . . ." His face registered horror. "In fact, I thought absolutely nothing more about it until Monday morning, when lo and behold, what should I receive in the mail but an envelope with a one hundred dollar bill inside."

"Did you keep the envelope?"

"No. But I must confess, I kept the money. Then later that day I received another telephone call from the same man. He reminded me I was to get the room for the following evening." He opened his hands. "And so, of course, I did. I followed his instructions to the letter. On Tuesday at exactly three thirty, after getting the room, I proceeded to the telephone booth in the hotel lobby. I placed the key in the yellow pages of the telephone book and left the building. At four o'clock I returned to the same booth. The key was gone, but in its place"—his hands began to work with imaginary paper—"I found another envelope." Julian looked up, unable to believe his good fortune. "Inside was yet *another* one hundred dollar bill!"

"Then what did you do?"

"My dear fellow. I did what I had agreed to do. I called

Elizabeth and told her to meet me in room five eleven at ten thirty that evening." His hands opened a second time, as though to add depth to what he said. "My man promised to send me the final payment in the mail. But I doubt very much that he will."

"Hadn't you heard about Gretchen Flanders?" I asked.

"Of course. But it didn't *occur* to me that this man . . . Mr. Tree, I believed it to be Elizabeth's husband. I thought it all quite—poetic."

I got up more quickly than I had expected and turned my back on him. "Richard? Any questions?"

Hunter sat down and rested his notebook on the table. "You say you threw the first envelope away?"

"Yes."

"What about the second one?"

"I'm afraid I disposed of it as well."

"Do you have either of the hundred dollar bills?"

"Good heavens no. I changed them into twenties as soon as I got them."

"Where were they changed?"

Thoms pursed his lips and stared at the ceiling. "The first one at a liquor store on Colorado Boulevard—let me think—The Thumb. The second one at a bank on Stout Street, near the Arena Hotel."

"Remember who changed them?"

"An Oriental girl waited on me at the bank, but I doubt if she would remember me." He smiled with perhaps too much modesty. "The man at the liquor store should, however. I've made quite a number of purchases there."

"Can I get a photograph of you?"

"Of course. Mike, would you ask my aunt to give this gentleman one from her scrapbook?"

"All right."

"One more question," Hunter said, reviewing his notes. "Can you describe the man's voice?"

"Assured, Midwestern, business-like. He sounded exactly the way I would expect a junior high school principal to sound."

160

It was sticky and hot outside, and the air an exhaust-tinted blue. My face felt oily, as though I'd tried to clean it with a towel dipped in butter. "We ought to hang it on Thoms," Hunter said. "The creepy bastard."

Neither one of us said very much as we rode in his car toward Leetsdale Drive, until he said he'd learned some funny things about Cora. She may have been a "very competent geologist," but according to his investigation she'd also been a crook.

She'd been a brilliant high school student apparently, but ran away from home to avoid prosecution for theft. She'd worked part-time as a checker in the grocery store her father managed, selling food to her friends for less than the purchase price, then collecting back part of what they'd saved.

It didn't sound too crooked to me and I said so. But Hunter wasn't finished. She put herself through college the same way, he said, but on a bigger scale. She'd work as a salesperson in a department store and net two or three hundred dollars a month. Usually she quit and moved on to another job before suspicion focused on her, but twice she was caught. The first time she was allowed to make restitution and no charges were brought, and the second time the DA dismissed the case for lack of evidence. "This wasn't spur-of-the-moment shop-lifting, Mr. Tree. It was a calculated scheme. She developed it and was good at it, and in my book that makes her a crook."

"Didn't she work for an oil company in Wyoming?"

"Yeah. Wyoco Oil. Something fishy about that, too. Worked six months and quit, but gets a glowing recommendation and gets snapped up immediately by Drake."

"What's fishy about that?"

"Wyoco is one of the big five oil companies in the United States. Right?"

"Yes."

"Why would they give her such a super recommendation when she quit after six months?"

"Spell it out," I said.

161

"A big company like that loses money on people who don't stay. They all have their own way of doing things, takes at least six months to get a new person trained. Cora had just come out of college, too. You'd think that with her quitting so soon they wouldn't be so generous."

"Mmm."

We found the address on Leetsdale Drive and Hunter parked the car. Neither one of us wanted to get out. The house we saw was tidy looking with brightly painted trim and a carefully kept lawn, somehow it looked as though it had been scrubbed in soap.

Sergeant Flanders had a glass of scotch in his hand when he opened the door, and we sat around his kitchen table listening as the children played in the back yard. He was a small, sunburned man with pain-dulled eyes and a sensitive mouth, whose hands looked like blunt instruments. The last three fingers of his left hand were missing above the second joint.

I let Hunter ask the questions. His wife had left the house about ten on Saturday night, to help a German-born girl friend study for her citizenship exam, Flanders thought. He'd always thought she taught two or three nights a week. She never left the house until the kids were in bed though, or until she'd fixed him dinner and made him comfortable. Then about eleven thirty Saturday night, he found out she'd been murdered.

Here he thought she was just an old-fashioned girl. The only good thing about it, he said, was the fact he didn't care. In fact, he was glad. Gretchen had over five thousand dollars in a savings account under an assumed name, and a lawyer told him it was his. So he was glad. He'd get the goddam house sold, he said, and then fuck it. He'd think of something.

I could see Timothy when we left, floating in front of me and weeping like a soft-headed jackass. I felt a little like patting him on the head.

Toward evening we found Farre at his home in South Denver. He had the set-in-his-ways jaw of an old-time farmer, who resented the intrusion but was too courteous to say so. He'd known about Elizabeth's affair, he said, but hadn't quite decided how to handle it. She refused to tell him anything and he hadn't gotten around to calling Thoms. In a way he'd just ignored it, hoping his wife would come to her senses.

The police had called him out of a school board meeting Tuesday night, he told us, not long after eleven o'clock. It was Elizabeth all right. That silly robe was draped over one leg as though she was a middle-aged movie star trying to look sexy, and she'd been strangled. He hoped the whole sordid business might serve as a lesson to someone.

When we drove away, I asked Hunter if he'd like a drink. "Sure," he said. "Only . . ."

"Only what?"

"Well, I hate to get you started. No offense."

I laughed, oddly enough. "I'll be damned. I didn't know you cared."

"Funny thing to say, Mr. Tree, but I really do."

We found a bar on Colfax that served Kosher corned beef sandwiches, and my first impulse was to tell everyone there to go on back to New Jersey. Then I thought, what the hell. The lead from their exhausts is no different than the lead from mine. I felt so charitable I even ordered one and found that by putting on horseradish I could eat it.

"What're we doing, Mr. Tree?" Richard asked, taking a potato chip off my plate and stuffing it in his mouth. On another day I might have told him to get his own damned potato chips, but that day, strangely enough, I didn't. It made me feel less lonely. "I mean, here the police think they've got the nut, but we keep right on looking like whoever got those ladies is our man."

"He is."

"I know what you're thinking," Hunter said. "Wicked adulteresses. The so-called madman killed Gretchen and Elizabeth, you think he'll go for Sharon next. Only . . ."

"Go ahead."

"Isn't there more than the notes, Mr. Tree? Sure, they look like the one with Chambers, but is that enough?"

"Let me ask you to think a little, Richard. If it gets too hard, say so." I hadn't intended to be sarcastic, but recognized it might have sounded a little harsh, so I smiled. "How many people would you say get murdered in Denver in a year?"

"Two or three a week, I suppose. Depends on whether payday comes on Friday."

"That would develop about a hundred bodies a year, right? Now how many of them are murdered in out-of-the-ordinary ways?"

He tasted his beer and thought it over. "Not many, especially in two weeks. But it could happen, Mr. Tree. Things go in streaks."

I drained my glass and signaled the waitress for two more. "True. But when a person is strangled—especially by what everyone thinks is a religious maniac—wouldn't you expect to find something to evidence hate, or rage, or passion on the part of the killer?"

"He choked the hell out of Flanders," Hunter said. "Broke a couple bones in her neck."

"Then laid the note over her navel and got away. A bizarre action—the picture of a nut—but if he is, he's a very efficient one. How many nuts are that efficient?"

"Jesus. Why kill half the goddam women in Denver just to get at Sharon?"

"That shouldn't be too hard, even for you," I said, and smiled again. "It'd be too obvious, just now, to kill her. The police would look for motive and that could bring the whole thing crashing down. So he has to provide a very obvious motive."

"Why not an accident?"

"Accidents don't always work."

"Okay. So Mr. X is out there somewhere, stalking Sharon. He's gonna make her murder look like the murders of Gretchen and Elizabeth, then everybody'll think she was killed by a kook and no one will know why she was really killed."

"Good for you."

"So all we got to do is figure out where he's gonna hit Sharon, be there when he tries, catch him in the act. Right?" He sipped his beer. "What a neat ending."

"He'll try to kill her Friday night," I said.

"How do you figure?"

"She has to be dead before she can testify, because he can't take a chance on her. That means before Monday. Flanders was killed Saturday night around eleven and three days later—Tuesday night—the Farre woman. Also around eleven."

"Three more days is Friday? Is that it?"

"Careful, Richard. You'll strain those muscles in your head."

"Damn it, Mr. Tree, can't you . . ."

"Sorry, Richard," I said. And I really was sorry. "Everything else is in threes, and it seems so obvious. Three robes, three murders, three wicked adulteresses—probably three notes—and all of it patterned after the Holy Trinity of Father, Son, and Holy Ghost."

He rubbed his nose. "Jesus. Mr. X may be sane, but this is weird."

"How many men are tailing Sharon?" I asked.

"Two teams. Makes four men. Even I can figure that out."

"Can you get a back-up team?"

"Yeah." He looked tired and glanced at his watch. "Even with a back-up, she could lose us if she tried."

He wanted to leave, so I picked up the check, even though I'd liked to have stayed and talked. On the way to my office, I told him I was going to fly to Casper the next day, but would be back on Friday in time for the "neat ending." I wanted to find out why Wyoco Oil had given Cora such a fine send-off, I said. And if Mr. X killed Sharon before I got back, Richard should take it in his stride. I've been wrong before, I told him.

16

Casper, Wyoming, is a beautiful town from the air. It is contained within boundaries—unlike Denver, which spreads over the prairie like an oil slick—so at least you can tell where Casper quits and the country around it begins. From the air in the summer, the countryside looks green and open.

But the wind blows in Casper. My dad used to say they had built the town into the wind, and if it ever stopped, the whole place would fall over.

Wyoco Oil had its own building on the fringes of the downtown area. It was new, made of tinted glass and steel girders, and stood seven stories high. From the top floor, you could see cottonwood trees along the sandy bottoms of the North Platte; and off to the south, the Laramie Mountains.

Mr. Sheldon Gaddes sat behind his executive desk, rocking slowly in his chair like a cowboy on a horse. His expression was noncommittal, as though he had a rope in his hand but didn't want the steer to know he could throw it. He wore a string tie and a short-sleeved shirt, and every part of him I could see was tanned—even his head. "Tell the truth, Mr. Tree, we expected to hear from the Denver DA about her. But it's confidential information."

166

"If you were going to tell it to the DA, why can't you tell me?"

"Just that we always cooperate with the authorities. At least when we can."

He sounded like the prime minister of a foreign nation, and as the representative of one of the Big Five, he probably was. I decided to treat him as though I were an emissary from a friendly government. "The DA isn't the only one who represents the people of Colorado, Gaddes. I do too. I have the same power he does when it comes to subpoenas." He didn't appear particularly moved by my words. "What I don't understand is why you'd force me to use it. Sure as hell it'd result in a lot of publicity—another oil company, taking a typically horseshit position—and what difference does it make to you?"

He smiled like a good-old-boy, but I knew better. "Tell you what, Tree. You just go ahead and ask your questions and we'll see if there's a problem. What the hell. There probably isn't even a problem."

I settled back, as though relieved by his attitude. "First, I'd like to confirm when she worked for you, and how long, and so forth."

"You wait here a minute," he said, getting up and walking across the deep brown rug for the door. "I'll get her file. Like some more coffee?"

"Fine."

When he came back he didn't hand me the file, and I didn't reach for it. The information checked. The Shannon girl had graduated with honors from the University of California at a time when Wyoco was anxious to hire qualified women as geologists. They started her in their Research and Exploration division. Everything in her file indicated she was a highly motivated young woman; her performance ratings were uniformly high; they were sorry to see her leave.

"She worked for you six months, didn't she?"

He searched through the file. "Yes."

167

"And after that went to work for Dolores Petroleum?"

"That's right too."

"Did they ask for a recommendation?"

"Yep. She put us down as a reference and her supervisor, Johnny Oakes, wrote a really nice letter."

"Can I see it?"

"Sure." He took the letter out of the file and handed it across the desk.

The letter exuded sincerity, warmth, and personal concern. It portrayed her as devoted, hard-working, and extremely competent. "I don't get it," I said. "If you felt that good about her, why did you let her go?"

"We just plain couldn't keep her here is all. She had this other opportunity and she never really did like Casper. It's awful small up here, especially compared to a place like Denver. Aren't even forty thousand people in the whole town." He took some coffee. "Great, if you hunt and fish, but it gets cold in the winter and she just plain didn't like it."

"No hard feelings?"

"Naw. You'll find, in spite of what you hear, management isn't like that any more. Doesn't make sense. Keep 'em if they're happy, but if they aren't, let 'em go. Creates a better atmosphere all around."

"Had she ever been involved in anything shady?"

He glanced at me sharply. "Like what?"

"Anything dishonest?"

He went carefully through the file. "No mention of anything like that."

"Did you know she'd been charged with theft in California?"

"Cora? I don't believe it." I told him what Hunter had told me. "Well, I'll be damned," he said.

"What can you tell me about William Drake?" I asked.

"Kind of a whiz kid. From an old oilman family, lots of money, full of big ideas. Short on experience, though."

"Is he honest?"

"Now what the hell do you expect me to say?"

"Off the record," I said. "Gossip." He looked at me as though he wondered how much I knew. "Could he have been led down the old garden path by a pretty crook?"

"Maybe if I knew exactly what you're driving at . . ."

"She did an assay on some land owned by Great Mesa. But I understand there's another one—also by her—that reaches a different conclusion." Gaddes grinned at me. "You heard about that?" I asked.

"I've got copies of both, Tree," he said. "As if you didn't know."

"When did you get them?"

"The first one about six months ago, the second one, yesterday." He continued to grin. "Poor old Billy Drake sure got his tit caught in a wringer!"

"How do you mean that?"

"Well, the dumb bastard. Either he or Cora—and I just don't think she'd do it—phonied the data in that first assay. Billy tried to buy that land for one helluva lot less than it's worth."

"How did you get the reports?"

"Now wait a minute, Tree. Wasn't just Wyoco. *All* the majors got them. We've known about that land—partly because of the lawsuit but partly because there's enough water on it to develop it—and water is always a problem when you're dealing with shale."

"I still don't know how you got those reports."

He tugged at his ear, then smiled. "Guess it can't hurt, when everyone in the industry knows anyway. When those radicals started giving Dix a bad time, at least three of the majors tried to buy him out—as much to keep him from giving the industry a bad name as anything else. But that old bastard wanted a hundred million dollars! Well, you don't spend that kind of money on a man's say-so. Standard finally wormed out of him the fact that Dolores Petroleum had done an assay, and he gave them permis-

169

sion to get a copy—like pulling all his teeth, I heard—and we got it from them.

"So then Dix tried to tell everybody the report was wrong, but it sure as hell looked right to *my* people. We know something about the shale land about a mile north of there and it's so salinized it's worthless."

"I don't follow you."

"Know anything about oil shale, Tree?"

"A little," I said. "The valuable stuff is actually kind of a wax, isn't it? You find it in a rock called organic marl-stone?"

He nodded. "Kerogen, it's called—petroleum, just as much as regular oil—but it didn't get formed the same way. Both are deposits of organic matter from swamps, jungles, animals, and so forth, and both lay on the ground and decomposed and got covered by sand and all until they became layers of earth. But the so-called oil shale got lifted up by earthquakes and things before the pressure of the earth could turn it into a liquid. So it just got turned into kind of a gum.

"Now lots of times you'll find salinization in regular oil. If the oil pool, or oil shale bed, got formed in a salt water sea or some such, then there's bound to be a lot of salinization. It won't hurt an oil pool particularly because it's dissolved into the oil, and when you get the oil out it's easy to separate off the salt. But it's a different story with oil shale. Shale just plain isn't commercial if much of the kerogen has been displaced by salt. You need at least thirty gallons of petroleum to a ton of rock, and that stuff north of Great Mesa runs fifteen to twenty-five, and as far as present mining methods are concerned, that's the same as not having any."

"Dix's land is better than the land north of it? How can that be?"

"Not unusual at all. The salinization bed just doesn't extend into his land."

"Then you think Cora Shannon falsified the assay?"

170

"No. I think Billy Drake did." He stroked his chin. "She wasn't convicted of anything in California, was she?"

"How did you get this last report?"

"Dix sent it to us yesterday. Crazy old bastard. I can see him, jumping up and down and clicking his heels."

"How do you know *it* isn't a phony?" I asked.

"We called Drake. He gave us some song and dance about how the first one was inaccurate and his people just found it out, so they sent out a new one." Gaddes shook his head. "Billy-boy's fightin' like hell to wriggle out of something. I'd like to know what, and was kind of hoping maybe you could tell me."

"Sorry." I got up. "You were really disappointed to see her leave. Is that right?"

"That's right, Tree." He held her personnel file as though it were a shield. "She was one hell of a gal and we hated to lose her."

Barry Hanes was a judge in Casper, and it seemed to suit him. I'd gone through law school with Barry and in those days he'd been barrel-chested and strong. He still looked as though he could toss you into the next county, although he might have trouble getting his hands on you. The barrel was now as massive as an oil drum.

"You old son of a gun!" he said to me, grinning hugely. It made me feel good. "I heard you'd gotten weird, turned into a lush—Jesus! You're as skinny now as you ever were!"

We sat in his chambers and even though it took a while to get to it, I didn't mind. Barry had never been noted for his intellect, but hearing him spin yarns is more fun than reading a book by Charlie Russell. Finally: "What's up, Nathan? You didn't come here to fish. The Platte won't fish until you follow it almost back to Colorado."

"Ever hear about Cora Shannon, Barry?" It wasn't an improbable question. Most of the professional people in Casper are men, and they all belong to the Elks Club. They do a lot of gossiping down there.

171

"Yeah," he said, "I even touched her once. Man, what a beautiful thing."

"How come she quit working for Wyoco?"

"She didn't quit. She was canned." He stuck a cigar in his mouth and lit it. "Aren't you representing the guy who killed her? Put her in a waterbed, didn't he? What the hell would a guy do *that* for?"

"Why was she canned?"

"I'll tell you, but you can't use me as a source."

"Fair enough."

"She was selling confidential information to other oil companies. Wyoco even filed a criminal complaint against her for grand theft—I know because I was scheduled to hear the preliminary—but then they withdrew the charge. Seems she'd had a little affair with old Shelley Gaddes, is what I heard, so she kind of had him by the ying-yang." He smiled. "Man, I bet it was worth it."

Gaddes wasn't so nice the second time. I told him I'd checked the records at the County Court and found that Wyoco had filed, then withdrawn, a criminal complaint against Cora Shannon for grand theft. I even gave him the docket number. Then I told him I'd gone to the Elks Club for a drink and learned he'd had an affair with the lady. Was that why the complaint had been dismissed?

He acknowledged that it was.

"But you had to get her out of Casper, so you gave her a letter of recommendation, and probably told her to try Drake because of his inexperience?"

"Something like that."

I had a hunch and there was nothing to lose by trying it out. "Why did you keep her on the payroll?"

"How the hell did you find out about that?" He wiped his hand across his head. "You can ruin me, Tree. Flatass ruin me."

"You haven't answered my question."

"She was blackmailing me. I had more to lose than she

172

did and she knew it. So I continued her salary for six months, which was the only way I could come up with the five thousand dollars she said I owed her."

"I don't believe you, Gaddes. You kept her on because she was still working for you."

He looked scared. "What the hell are you talking about?"

"You knew what she could do for you. If she sold Wyoco's secrets to others, what was to keep her from selling Drake's secrets to you?"

"Honest to God, Tree. We don't operate that way," he said.

The flight from Casper was held up because of high winds, and I didn't get back until four o'clock Friday morning. I sat in my office and stared at the bottle on my desk.

The result was a foregone conclusion, but the joy of succumbing comes in teasing yourself first with temptation. It's like illicit sex, I thought. The pleasure requires conscience and morals and the delicious awareness that what you are going to do is a sin. The seal on the bottle broke easily and I poured some whisky into my coffee mug. Lucky for me I have a conscience, I thought. Otherwise I couldn't get the most out of a drink.

The whisky tasted good, like burned honey, and the warmth of it spread to my hands and feet. I swirled the whisky in my mug and watched the currents form a pattern in the liquid. At least this time I'd had the sense to doubt the obvious—which might account for why it had taken so long to understand. You need to be selective about which obvious things you doubt, because some things are so obvious they're part of the background, and then they aren't obvious at all. Still, they are there to trip over, if you get close enough.

I knew now why Cora had been planted in the waterbed, and if there was time for another burglary, I might

173

have found the proof. But there wasn't because tonight was the night.

I put the cap on the whisky and put it away, even though I hadn't had enough to sleep. I didn't want to wind up in a cave. Then I got in bed and tried to shut my eyes, but the lids kept jumping open, so I stared in the halflight at the ceiling. Sometimes you see better with your eyes closed, I thought, and there must have been a few things I didn't want to see.

I'd like to know where he'll try to kill her, I thought. Maybe that's what I don't want to see.

17

"You gotta be kidding, Mr. Tree," Hunter said. He sat behind his desk at attention, as though the general of the army had just walked in.

I was tired, and it tends to make me nasty. "Damn it, Richard, I'm not kidding," I said.

He reached over and flipped the switch on his intercom. "Honey, can anyone who isn't working do a tail?"

"Everybody's out, Mr. Hunter."

"Anderson's on that Boatwright case, isn't he? He can dog on that a couple days. Bring him in." He flipped the system off. "I can work with Anderson; we can tail him if we can find him. But why not have him picked up?"

A nice young man, I thought, but his head is solid bone. "There isn't any proof. When he tries to kill her, we'll have proof."

"I mean, take that creepy psychologist," he said. "I can see *him* doing it. Alone that night with the girl, winds up doing something weird, and he's strange enough to put her in a waterbed, too. Then a psychologist, you know, natural for him to invent a madman to kill Sharon."

"Think a moment, Richard," I said patiently. "If he'd done it, wouldn't he be satisfied with leaving her body in the waterbed? And if for some odd reason he was taken

175

with the urge to expose it to view at Garver's party, why would he involve Sharon? He was at the party himself. He could 'accidentally' slosh around on the waterbed without any help from her."

"What about Pete Garver then? Pete wasn't there that night."

"I recognize there are exceptions, but generally people require reasons for their actions. What reason did Pete have to kill the Shannon girl?"

"So you think it was for money, pure and simple. Right?"

I thought of the gardener and how he'd laughed the last time I'd seen him. The thing that made the fellow laugh was that Tim had already been executed. "It's never pure and simple," I said.

"You know, Mr. Tree, I used to hear how the major oil companies'd buy you out, kill you, for inventing engines that don't use gasoline. My old man'd swear by those tales. I can see Wyoco Oil or some big outfit scheming and plotting the whole thing to ruin a guy like Garver—bet he's cost them a bundle—and at the same time kill off a defector like Cora. But I can't see one guy, know what I mean? It's too big, like a conspiracy, like what kept my old man in debt all his life. Know what I mean?"

"You're trying to tell me what you mean." Richard's expression suffered through a transformation of some kind, which I'd expected but couldn't get any pleasure out of. "When you mix two people and make them privy to that kind of information—especially when one of them was slightly crooked to start with—what can you expect?"

The peculiar static sound that lets you know someone in another world is listening in came on. "Mr. Hunter? Andy broke his leg last night. Shall I tell him to come in anyway?"

Hunter's expression suffered through another transformation, then he took a deep breath. "No," he said into the speaker. "Just send the dummy a get-well card." He leaned on his desk. "Sonuvabitch."

"Can you do it alone?" I asked.

"He'd lose me walking down the street."

"I'll work it with you then."

He looked at me as though he wasn't sure. "Okay. You're kind of conspicuous though, Mr. Tree. You got a shirt that isn't white?"

He was in the Oilmen Club Building. Hunter sat in his car across the street from the main entrance, and I was slumped in my truck in the alley. We were about as inconspicuous as Pike's Peak, I thought, but Hunter seemed satisfied with the arrangement and I didn't know any better. I ached with tiredness but still couldn't close my eyes, and now and then would have a nip from the bottle under the seat. "How you doing, Mr. Tree?" Hunter asked. His voice came over the portable radio system he'd installed in my truck.

"Fine."

"Feel like talking?"

"No." That doesn't sound very friendly, I thought. "But I'll listen."

He laughed, then started talking, and it had a pleasant sound. I quit listening to what he said, but could hear the inflections and knew when to grunt.

You're getting mellow, Tree, I thought, as I had a small tug. It doesn't seem to bother you that the Hunters are in town. In fact, bring them on, I thought. Let there be pavement as far as the eye can see. You can't turn over rocks without finding ants, and they're probably under the pavement too. So flood the place with people, because it should make a better world for the ants.

I put the cap back on. Maybe you've had enough, Tree, I thought.

The sun no longer made shadows on the street, but it was still light out, even though most of the cars driving by had on their lights. I felt peculiar, as though Carruthers had slipped me one of his pills, and stared beyond the brick canyon walls into the slice of deepening sky.

"What?" I said. Hunter's voice had taken an urgent turn.

"I said she ditched 'em. Just got the call on my other radio. She had a cab waiting in the alley by the side door of a movie."

"Get the cab company."

"Won't do any good, but I'll try. She'll be long gone before we can get to wherever she's being taken."

"Well, we still have . . ."

"He's been in there too long. I better take a look."

"Good idea."

A minute or so later a young executive type strode briskly out the door I was watching, glanced at me, then marched smartly down the alley in the other direction. It couldn't be, I thought. The man was too short. Then a dog wandered down the cement path, urinating on everything. The creature might be smarter than people, I thought. It could have been a comment.

Then Hunter bumped through the door and ran up to my truck. "I can't find him, Mr. Tree," he said.

It was dark and I couldn't turn on the light, but could see well enough to recognize the room. I walked softly to the kitchen and opened the door, then stood in a shadow where I could see without being seen, and waited.

The pistol in my hand felt heavy and I wondered, if it came to it, if I could. I'd shot two Nazis during my generation's war, and the second one hadn't been so bad, but the first time I threw up.

In a way it was funny, standing there, waiting and wondering if I was right. I almost fell asleep. The whisky in my body seemed to have passed on through to my soul, and I felt gentle and relaxed as I waited there, possibly to kill.

And then I heard a quiet clink as someone fit a key into a lock.

The door swung open, admitting light from the hall, and for a moment the silhouette of a huge man filled the space. It shut immediately and I thought I might have imagined it, but after a while I could see him—a gray shadow against a black one—standing without moving by the door.

Five minutes later there was the same tinkle of metal on metal, and the door opened again. Another silhouette—this time a woman—who seemed to leave the door open a dramatic moment more than was needed, as though to give the cameras a chance to focus.

"Hello?" she said.

"Hello."

She giggled. "Kind of exciting," she whispered. "Did you bring . . ."

Her voice stopped and I heard feet shuffling, as though someone at a movie house was letting someone else through the aisle. I turned on the light.

"Drop her, Dix," I said.

He had Sharon by the throat, and turned and stared at me. But his grip didn't loosen and Sharon's eyes were popping out of her head. "Tree?"

"Damn it, Dix, stop!" I said, moving out of the kitchen and aiming the gun at his face.

His grip loosened and Sharon reached for the powerful hands around her throat. Then Dix seemed to come to another decision. "You're going to have to kill me, young man," he said. "Your father would understand." His fingers closed once more and Sharon's back and head arched in agony.

I could have shot him in the leg, but he had to be stopped, and, besides, I knew what he meant. I obliged him and shot him in the head.

I sat on Garver's waterbed and waited for the storm.

179

"What the hell did you do that for?" Charlie Riggs demanded.

"Professional courtesy," I said. "She needed a lawyer so I got her one." Charlie was upset because I'd called Gerry Ashe before calling the police, and Gerry had taken Sharon to the hospital. They'll never make a case on her now, I thought, Gerry will see to that; but it didn't matter. She'll have a sore neck and that's enough.

"Some pal *you* are. Jesus Christ. Should've left you on the floor that day in court."

"Come on, Charlie," I said, and wondered if my eyes would close if they had the chance. "I've solved four murders for you. Isn't that . . ."

"Five, if you count Dix." He dragged up a chair. "Nobody's here. I don't have a bug. I want to know what happened."

I started out by telling him how a man like Dix must have felt—a pioneer oilman whose life revolved around a vision that was finally coming true—when he learned it never could, because the land it depended on was worthless.

There was a lot Charlie didn't know that I had to explain. He didn't know about the assay reports the Shannon girl had done for Dolores Petroleum, so I told him about them. All three of them.

The first one—the real one—might have been destroyed. If it was anywhere, Dix had it in his office; but it wasn't needed. The land itself would prove what it had said.

When Cora Shannon did the work, Dix undoubtedly followed her around like a puppy on a leash. Her findings must have galled the old man's soul. But with the right kind of assay report, he could at least sell the land to Drake, so he persuaded the girl to present Drake with a false one.

That was the report everyone thought was real. According to it, Dix's land was worth almost what he had always thought it was worth—but that turned out to be more than

180

Drake could pay. So then Drake went to work on the girl. He begged and pleaded with her to write a phony report, which would show the values to be an amount he could afford.

Kind of funny up to that point, I said. The Shannon girl would have reported the wrinkle in their scheme back to Dix, and Dix jumped on it. He'd been in the oil business long enough to know something about promotion; and when the "truth" got out—and Dix would make sure the first false report got found—that in itself would create interest in his land. So he told her to go ahead and write an assay that would satisfy Drake.

Then he went about selling the land. He started by strip-mining a ridge in a way calculated to bring the wrath of the environmentalists down on his head, and they performed exactly as they were expected to. They brought suit, stopping the operation. Dix—now the disillusioned old man—let it be known the government was an interfering ass, and if he lost he was so disgusted he'd sell.

The perverse old son of a bitch, I said. If the Fates saw fit to do him dirty, he'd just pay them back. The next thing he had to do was lose his case. He was so obvious in his efforts it took a while for me to trip over it, I said—and it's so obvious too that Dix was the only one who was getting anything.

"You mean he lost that case against Clear Sky on purpose?" Charlie asked.

"Yes," I said. "But somewhere along the line, it quit being funny. Dix realized what would happen if his partner suddenly acquired a few million dollars and then later her report turned out to be a fraud. You can see how that might look, can't you, Charlie?"

"Damn it, Nathan, don't start in on me."

"Sorry. Just trying to be nice."

I went on to tell him how Dix then decided to take advantage of the fact the Shannon girl was in Garver's camp. It didn't matter whose idea it was to put her there: her own, or Drake's, or Dix's: but there she was, sleeping on Garver's waterbed, reporting back to Dix as well as Drake.

"What was there to report?"

"A whole lot of gossip, Charlie. Phillip'd had an affair with his sister-in-law . . ."

"The one Ashe just took to the hospital?"

"Yes. Cora gossiped about the waterbed, too, apparently, which gave Dix his big idea. He was in a spot. If he sold his land for millions of dollars on the basis of either of the fraudulent assays, suspicion would focus on him once the fraud was discovered. He had to get rid of the writer of the reports, and do it so no one would guess why. Sure as hell, pinning it on an environmentalist hit the old man as the perfect solution: so neat as to be positively righteous."

"Yeah, but why put her in the waterbed?"

"Timing." My eyes lost their focus, and Charlie had two heads. "For the frame to work, she had to be killed while she was still living with Garver. But Dix had to lose the case too, and he wasn't about to trust Garver to win it without help. That's why he wanted the girl to stay with Garver as long as possible. He knew, though, that when the trial was over she'd leave. He also knew that if her body was found just before the trial—if the champion of the environmentalists was suddenly accused of murder—the publicity could have a disastrous effect on the case. It might even mean he'd win! So he put her in there, knowing he could arrange to have her body found as soon as he was certain he'd lost the case."

"How'd he arrange to do that?"

"Through the sister-in-law. He got her to tromp around on the waterbed at Garver's party. The oil business isn't that far from show business, Charlie. Dix knew if her body got discovered at one of Garver's parties, it'd create the kind of publicity he could use to sell the land."

"How'd he get the sister-in-law to help?"

I decided not to put too much strain on our friendship,

even though I'd talked to Sharon before Ashe arrived. "I don't know, exactly. It might have had something to do with the affair, or the woman spurned thing, or both. She wouldn't have gone along with murder though, Charlie. When she passed out that night at the party, it was genuine."

"You mean she didn't know the waterbed had a body in it? What the hell was she doing tromping around on it then?"

"Dix must have told her something else was in there."

"You talked to her before Ashe got here or you wouldn't have called Ashe, Nathan. What'd she tell you?"

"This is pure speculation, Charlie. But Dix might have told her he didn't know himself. He could have said some people had been hired to put something in there that would embarrass Garver."

"I gotta believe that shit?" He puffed angrily on a cigar. "Well, go on."

"The trouble with using Sharon was that it created another problem. It left a link between Dix and his scheme. That's why he killed Flanders and that Farre woman, and tried to kill Sharon tonight."

"What about Chambers?"

"Dix knew he couldn't put a body in the waterbed by himself, so he hired Chambers to help. Then after killing Cora, he killed Chambers—and was careful enough to make that one look like Garver too. Which wouldn't have been very hard. He probably got a key to the Clear Sky office from Cora, then typed the letter from Gavin Phillips about the gun."

Charlie got up. "Sharon Garver's an accomplice," he said. "Except for her, though, you're the only proof I got. You willing to testify?"

"No."

"What was she doing here tonight?"

"My guess is she thought Dix would give her some money to keep quiet."

"Your guess, huh?" He knocked some ashes on the rug. "How'd you know he was gonna kill her here?"

"I finally caught on to the pattern the so-called madman was using. Killing wicked adulteresses, where they'd met with their lovers."

We heard a commotion in the other room and suddenly the door broke open. Richard Hunter stood there like Horatio at the bridge, fiercely concentrating on his single purpose and seemingly unaware of the fact that two men were trying to pull him back. When he saw me, his face relaxed. "You okay, boss-man?"

He seemed genuinely relieved, and it made me feel odd. "I'm okay, muscle head," I said.

I sat in the truck, finishing the bottle and watching the sun come up. I'd been wondering what would happen to Mrs. Dix. "Woman," Robert had called her—but her name was Stella, and she had the grace to know it. I knew she'd be all right.

That old sour-hearted son of a bitch. I felt an affinity for the old dinosaur, but wondered about him too. It was possible he never knew what it was he hated. Maybe that's the common factor, I thought. Us dinosaurs don't know what to hate.

All at once a tiredness dropped on me like a heavy net and it was all I could do to crawl out of the cab of my truck and stagger for the steps to my apartment. Then someone took my elbow and helped me, even getting the key out of my hand and opening the door, and staying long enough to make sure I found the couch. "Easy, Mr. Tree," the little man said. "Take it easy."

A very understanding person, I thought, drifting toward a heavy, deep sleep. I knew who it was, too: I'd recognize him anywhere.

It was Timothy Pettersenn III.